sugar bush & other stories

Acknowledgements:

Earlier versions of some of these stories appeared in the following publications:

"Only Game in Town": 2002 edition of *Pearls*, the Douglas College Creative Writing Department anthology.

"Letters from the Pink Room": *Prism international* 40:2 (Winter 2002).

"Farm Report": *subTerrain*, Issue 33 (Winter 2001).

"Tourist": *Vancouver Courier*, December, 2002.

"Chicken Shack": *Vancouver Courier*, December, 2005.

I'm tremendously grateful to those who encouraged and supported me in the production of *Sugar Bush*—friends, teachers, editors, fellow writers, and Brian, who's all those things. Special thanks to my mentors at otherwords (RIP), undercurrents, and Sage Hill.

Sugar Bush
&
Other Stories

Jenn Farrell

Anvil Press / Vancouver

Anvil Press Inc.
P.O. Box 3008, Main Post Office
Vancouver, B.C. V6B 3X5 CANADA
www.anvilpress.com

LIBRARY AND ARCHIVES CANADA CATALOGUING IN PUBLICATION

Farrell, Jenn, 1971–

Sugar bush and other stories / Jenn Farrell.

ISBN: 1-895636-76-0

I. Title.

PS8611.A774S93 2006 C813'.6 C2006-905157-7

This is a work of fiction. Any resemblance to persons either living or deceased is purely coincidental.

Printed and bound in Canada
Cover illustration and design: Karen Klassen
Interior design & typesetting: HeimatHouse

Represented in Canada by the Literary Press Group
Distributed by the University of Toronto Press

The publisher gratefully acknowledges the financial assistance of the Canada Council for the Arts, the Book Publishing Industry Development Program (BPIDP), and the Province of British Columbia through the B.C. Arts Council and the Book Publishing Tax Credit.

table of contents

For Rob & Cypress

Only Game in Town

Emma's mud mask is starting to harden. She looks in the bathroom mirror, pokes at her cheek with an index finger. The clay dents slightly and then cracks, like the frosting on a cheap birthday cake. It's still wet in places, darker around her lips and nose. She decides to leave it on for a few more minutes and pads across the living room to change the CD. She walks carefully, her feet covered in a layer of Vaseline and plastic wrap under her pom-pom socks. She can feel the greasy plastic sliding around her toes. Emma returns to her reflection and works a brush through her ponytail. The early evening sun through the glass-block window catches the highlights, turning them almost white, like frost on a windowpane. If this were a Bret Easton Ellis novel, she thinks, she would be a *total hardbody*.

The dinner rush begins at the Greek restaurant downstairs. Emma can hear the noise in the kitchen and smell the roasting lamb. The owners rented the upstairs apartment to her the day she looked at it. The landlady and her husband gave her a quick walk-through while they told the histories of all their bad tenants—drugs and loud music, couples shouting and stomping above the lunch customers' heads. Emma filled out the application on the kitchen counter, paid first and last in cash. This, and her quiet, agreeable answers to their questions, seemed enough to assure them that she would be different.

She didn't have much to unpack, just a foamy and a sleeping bag, a couple duffle bags, and a few cardboard boxes, one full of tattered paperbacks and creased posters. She's stacked most of the books on the mantel above the long bricked-over fireplace, and stuck the posters up on the walls. She found a perfectly good old table in the alley on garbage day, and the last tenants left a couple of vinyl dinette chairs on the balcony, so she even has a proper kitchen. She has yet to prepare any food in it. Her fridge holds a twelve-pack of Diet Pepsi, a bag of baby carrots, and half an Oh Henry bar.

After her face is done, Emma puts on her denim miniskirt and new sleeveless white shirt with *Angel* in pink glitter across the front. So far, the best part of her new job is the clothing discount. She's expected to wear Le Chateau stuff while she's on duty, but gets forty percent off the first six things she buys each month. The other girls are nice, but Emma keeps her guard up. The boredom of retail exhausts her in a way that waiting tables never did: folding sweaters around plexiglas rectangles, tagging striped socks with the little plastic gun, reassuring thirteen-year-olds that their asses don't look fat in jeans. She's used to hustling for tips, flirting, waitress politics, and hung-over brunch shifts.

Emma misses waitressing. When she and Scott moved to downtown Hamilton from Dundas, she thought everything would change for them—he'd get steady work, she would have new friends to hang out with, and they'd stop fighting about the same stupid stuff . . . but it hadn't turned out that way. Even finding an apartment was a disaster. They couldn't agree on anything, but since it was his money they were using, he had the final say. The place he ended up getting was a street-level shoebox on King that Emma hated. Every day, kids peeked through the mail slot into their living room since they had gotten lucky the first time and caught her unpacking in her underwear.

After a few weeks, Scott still hadn't found work, but Emma had found her job at the Bistro the first day she went out with a stack of résumés. She hadn't thought it would be so easy, or that there would be so many cute guys working there, or that everyone would be so into hanging out together after work. When the manager said they were one big family, he wasn't kidding. One big incestuous family.

She turns to admire her profile in the mirror. *Nice tits*. Emma's got a lot of good features, but her boobs take the cake. She wears a bra because she has to at work, but tonight she doesn't bother. She likes the way the shirt is stretched so tight across them that they warp the word "angel" a little bit.

She considers calling a couple of the girls from the Bistro. They'd be glad to hear from her, would probably love to go out, but eventually the talk would turn to work stuff. Besides, maybe some of the guys would show up and she doesn't want to see any of them, especially Robbie. Not that she blames him. She blames herself, too many drinks every night, being bored. The night it happened, she'd had a fight with Scott before she left for work. "If moving was supposed to make everything better, how come everything is exactly the same?" she asked him, and he didn't have an answer.

The flirting with Robbie all night at the bar and the kissing in the parking lot had been the best part. The sex, not so much. It was the kind that you lied to your friends about the next day; made it sound more fun than it really was.

The TV blaring, spilled beer on the carpet, and corn chips sticking to her back. Even worse was her confession to Scott—she had expected him to yell, and secretly hoped he would throw her out, but instead he had put his head down in her lap and started to cry. He didn't even want her to leave. She packed her stuff and left anyway.

Emma hadn't realized how little she knew of the city until she was on her own. A job and apartment were easy enough to replace, but her few friends, the places she went, even her sleeping patterns had all revolved around Scott and her co-workers. Now it's almost like a new city. Streets she's never seen in the daylight, bars she's never been to, places she tries to avoid.

She decides to go to Lux, that new club that's supposed to be good. She'll go alone and see if she can't have some fun, meet some people. Not necessarily a guy, but that wouldn't be so bad either.

The club is getting packed already, and it's only ten-thirty. There's retro-'90s alternative music on the top floor, latex Marilyn Manson hold-outs dancing with their arms like tentacles. Not her thing. She heads back down to the main room, where some rock band is setting up their gear. Lots of blue-collar guys and jocks in baseball caps are standing around drinking draft in plastic Molson

Canadian cups. Emma imagines taking any one of these home with her, trying them on. Someone lean and hard without too much to talk about. She finds an empty table in a corner, not far from the stage, and sits with her back to the wall. She crosses and uncrosses her legs, keeps moving slightly, like bait. She orders the draft on special. It's flat and watery, and she wishes she'd ordered a cooler instead, but she has to be careful now that she doesn't have her tips to live off. She looks at her Hello Kitty watch. She decides she'll stay for a couple songs from the band, then maybe try another place down the street. A few guys have checked her out, but no one's approached her. She doesn't know whether to be relieved. She keeps smiling and tries to look like she's having fun, but not too much fun. Like she hangs out there all the time.

A guy in a wheelchair rolls up. He's holding two bottles of Corona in one hand, using the other to sidle up to her table. The sweaty beers clink together, and Emma is surprised at how quickly and smoothly he manoeuvers the chair.

"Hey!" he says, grinning. "Thought you might want a real beer. The draft here can kill you."

"Oh. Yeah. I mean, thanks." *A wheelchair? Oh Jesus,* she thinks.

"I'm Pete." He extends his paw.

"Emma."

"Emma," he says, looking into her eyes, "you are definitely the most fascinating woman in here."

He grips her hand warmly as she looks around. He's on her left, this Pete, blocking her only possible escape route. Her chair is wedged into the corner.

Pete seems to know everyone in the band, and nearly everyone in the bar besides. People wave and say hi. A scruffy looking guy plunks down at the table next to them. "Hey, Pete, haven't seen you in ages."

"I've been right here, man. Where the hell you been?"

"Did that contract up in Ingersoll for a couple months. Good money. This your old lady?" He nods towards Emma.

Pete laughs, winks at her. "Give her a minute, wouldya? I just met her."

Pete and the scruffy guy talk about the band. Pete tries to include her in the conversation, but she can't hear a word he's saying over the music. She leans forward though, nods in agreement. She checks him out when he's turned away from her, his long wavy hair and his Guatemalan patchwork jacket. She decides it's a look that says, *Look, baby, I may be forty and in a wheelchair, but I'm still a cool guy, I'm still hip*. Pity makes a home in her sternum, a small hard fruit.

Emma can barely hear him over the band, but he keeps

blabbing about music stuff, trying to impress her with his knowledge, which is a wasted effort. He's not a jerk or anything, but for a guy that called her fascinating, he doesn't seem to want to know much about her. But the waitress keeps the Coronas coming, and Pete keeps waving her hand away every time Emma gets her wallet out. Emma thinks that at least she has something to be grateful for.

"Do you wanna dance?" Pete tips his head towards the band, who are inciting the crowd to *get funky*.

"Sorry, what?"

"I said, do you want to dance, angel?"

Dancing. She pictures them on the dance floor, taking up most of the available space. Pete going around her in circles. Emma twirling in the centre. Pete popping a wheelie and everyone cheering.

"Not really in a dancing mood, thanks."

"Well, do you wanna get out of here for a bit, go get a coffee or something?"

"You know, I'm actually really tired. I think I should just go home, have an early night."

"Good idea. I'll head out with you."

They get to the entrance and Emma looks down the flight of stairs to the sidewalk. "Hey, Davy," says Pete to the bouncer, a bald black man in a sleeveless shirt.

Davy grins. "Hey, buddy, need a lift?" He hoists the

chair easily and walks down the stairs with Pete in his huge arms like a basket of dirty laundry. Emma watches from the top and considers, for a second, running back into the club and hiding in the ladies' room.

She can't imagine how to make a graceful exit from this night. The arithmetic of time + beer = expectations has bound her. She descends.

"Angel? Do me a big favour and push me for a minute? My arms are so tired . . . It's not far, I promise." Emma pushes him down King Street, hoping she doesn't get her toes caught under one of his wheels. They move through puddles of sickly fluorescent light cast by all-night pizza joints and donair shops.

At least from behind the chair, she doesn't have to look at his face. The only things Emma knows about guys in wheelchairs are what she's seen in the movies, and they're no help. She recalls a drunken Vietnam vet watching lesbian hookers. What movie was that, anyway? She wonders if he thinks he's going to hook up with her. Does his *thing* even work? She doesn't want to find out. Maybe he just wants to be her friend.

He lives in what must be one of Hamilton's grimiest high-rises. The lobby's decorated with mismatched cigarette-scarred sofas and dusty plastic palms. The chocolate brown shag carpet is old and matted like an ancient pelt. Emma's going to drop him at the lobby, but he looks back at her and says, "What, you're not even going to see me to my door?" in a mock offended way, but his face is so sad and lonely that she finds herself getting into the elevator with him. A rocker dude getting out of the elevator looks her over, then gives Pete the thumbs-up. Keep dreaming, Emma thinks.

Side by side in the bright light of the elevator, she finally gets a good look at his legs. They're little, like a child's. He's wearing tiny suede moccasins that stick out from his rolled-up jean cuffs. She imagines him trying to stand, his big head and torso supported by those withered legs, and wants to gag.

He touches her arm. "You okay there? Looks like you're gonna be sick, angel." Pete gently strokes her upper arm, like a father might. The elevator door opens, and Emma pushes him out into the hallway.

It's more like a motel room than an apartment. The unmade bed juts out from one wall, opposite a veneer dresser and a small TV set on a metal stand. There are stacks of music magazines everywhere: *Rolling Stone, Spin, Mojo.* There's a small bathroom off the main room. Emma knows, just from the feel of the wheelchair in her hands tonight, that it wouldn't fit through the narrow doorway.

Pete must have to get out of the chair and drag himself in with his arms. Which is what he's doing right now, pulling himself up onto the bed with surprising ease. He catches her staring and laughs.

"Thanks for the push," he says, "my arms are back to their old selves."

Pete pats the bed beside him, and Emma sits down. *If this were a Bret Easton Ellis novel,* she thinks, *someone would be holding a chainsaw by now.*

They talk some more about music, or he does anyway, and Emma nods a lot. He digs out some short articles and letters to the editor he's had published in magazines. She keeps sneaking glances at her watch, waiting for the right moment to say goodnight.

"Hey, Angel, would you do me a huge favour?"

"Hmm?"

"Would you rub my back for a bit? Sitting in that chair really messes with my spine. Please? Just for a minute?" Pete rolls over, and as he's pulling up the back of his shirt, says, "There's some baby powder on the nightstand. It'll make your hands slide easier."

She looks at his back and the faded black T-shirt bunched up around his thick neck. His skin is mottled, speckled brown on white, like an egg. Emma's reminded of killdeer's eggs, the nests in the open fields near her old house. The mother killdeer's loud squawks, her frenzied flapping and make-believe injury. She'd pretend to have a broken wing, invite an attack on herself instead of her babies, to lure predators away from the nest. The nest so exposed and vulnerable that the only defense is to be an easier target.

She reaches for the powder and sprinkles some onto his back. Her hands brush against him, and she feels his muscles tense and then release under her touch. She wonders why she's doing it as she strokes him. Does he try to pick up girls at bars every night and get them home? Does it usually work, or am I the only one who's this stupid? Emma realizes that no one knows where she is, and she's not expected at the store until tomorrow afternoon. For all she knows, Pete could have a knife or even a gun right there under his pillow. He could just roll over, point it at her and make her suck his dick. Instead, he emits a low, relaxed sigh.

She jerks away and jumps up from the bed. "I . . . I'm sorry, Pete, I can't do this. I have to go now, I'm really sorry . . ." She moves towards the door, backing away from Pete as though he's an unpredictable dog.

He rolls over onto his side, his shirt still hiked up, revealing a high round belly covered with fur. "What is it, Angel?"

"It's nothing, honestly. I just have to work super-early tomorrow and my boyfriend will be getting worried about me."

"So there's a boyfriend now, eh? You never said anything about a boyfriend."

"You never asked," Emma says, suddenly angry. "All you've done is talk about yourself all night, so how would you know? I just want to go home, okay?"

"What, you want money or something? How much? Fifty bucks? Sixty?"

"You think . . . you think I'm a *hooker*?"

He stares at her.

"You fucking perv," she says. "I only came up here—came all this way—because I felt *sorry* for you. You're just a . . . crippled loser."

"Sure I am," he says, nodding. "But what does that make you, getting free drinks off a cripple all night?" He smiles flatly, the corners of his mouth pulled sideways instead of up. "Cockteasing little bitch. Bet you think you're the only game in town, don'tcha?"

Emma grabs her bag from the nightstand and doesn't look up at him. She can hear him muttering as she closes the door behind her. She takes the stairs down from the eighth floor so she won't have to wait for the elevator outside his apartment.

On the street outside, Emma pants, pushing out every bit of stale air. She feels dizzy and sick. As she walks home, she keeps her head down, and hopes no one she knows saw her and Pete together. She manages not to throw up until she gets home.

Two days later, she dyes her hair purple. The girls at the store are delighted, and Emma doesn't tell them it's a disguise. She worries she's going to see Pete everywhere now, and she does. She doesn't go to Lux again, but there he is—at the pizza place across from the mall, in the book section of the Amity, handing out flyers in front of the record store. She sees him at night too, with other girls, young, good-looking ones who don't seem to be embarrassed or drunk. Every time, she tries not to duck her head, to keep her brow calm and unfurrowed and her eyes level, but he just looks right through her, like he's never seen her before.

Tourist

It was your first time on a plane, but despite the novelty, the flight seemed long. The descent into Vancouver was unmarked by any break in the clouds: the shapeless grey mist simply continued until you touched down. You decided there, still with your baggage in the overhead compartment, that you weren't going to stay. From a payphone, you called a friend of a friend in Victoria, who came and rescued you the following day from the cheapest of the airport hotels. Waiting in her car at the Tsawwassen ferry terminal, you shared a joint, damp and oily. You went too hard on it, forgot what province you were in, and had difficulty climbing the stairs after the boat was loaded. As you stood in line at the cafeteria trying not to appear stoned, the ferry began to move: it shuddered and creaked, rattling the dishes, sending vibrations up your legs.

"Is it like this for the whole way?" you asked too loudly of your companion, and the people around laughed with what you were sure was derision. *Tourist*.

The friend of a friend let you stay in her apartment, which was also her art studio. The space was cluttered with easels and stretched canvasses. There was no spare room or couch for you, so you ended up sharing the bed of her son. In the middle of the night, he fumbled with your breast and pressed his twelve-year-old boy body against you as you slept. You woke, first confused, then rigid with panic, pretended to be dreaming, thrashed about and rolled over. He returned to his side of the bed, and you squeezed your eyes closed, smoothed your breath. The next day you went to a sporting goods store and bought an air mattress with your meagre savings, and set it up in the entryway of the studio.

After a few late nights of beer and easy chatter, the friend of a friend became a friend in her own right. She offered to let you stay in the studio rent free for a month in exchange for keeping on eye on her son, helping him with his homework, and tidying up.

"Just until you get settled," she said, raising her glass.

You swept the splintered studio floor, taking care not to stroke the broom's bristles against the wet paintings leaning against the walls. Scrubbed the toilet. Used your suitcase as a nightstand.

Victoria reminded you of a trip you took as a child through the loosely strung necklace of tourist-trap towns ringing Lake Ontario. This place, too, looked like an overgrown train set. You walked around the city, trying too hard to make it your own. There was a lot of coffee, but no donuts. Your clothes were a dead giveaway—the plaid shirts and boy's jeans you bought in Wawa looked like grunge-rocker castoffs here. People your age wore flared corduroy trousers and skintight T-shirts with glittery racecars on them. Everyone was a hundred times more beautiful than you. You would never make any friends.

You went to the Goodwill store to find some new clothes and found a weathered Kangol hat, burgundy and soft, for a dollar. You were making your way towards the cash counter when a very old Chinese man approached you.

"Excuse me," he said, in an almost impenetrable accent. "Do you have the screaming pants?"

"I'm sorry, I don't work here," you answered, shaking your head, but he asked again, taking your arm in a gentlemanly fashion.

"Excuse me, do you have the screaming pants?"

While you struggled to imagine what the screaming pants were, you twisted the brim of your hat in your hands as though it was a steering wheel and you were driving far away. You continued to shake your head helplessly, his earnest face searching yours. Finally a much younger woman appeared behind him, placed her hands on his shoulders.

"He is looking for the swimming trunks," she said. You wanted to tell her that you were ashamed you didn't understand, that you didn't really know any Asian people. That Wawa's only contribution to Chinese culture was a restaurant that served greasy egg foo yung. But you smiled weakly and slunk out with the hat still in your hands and nobody stopped you and you didn't realize that you'd forgotten to pay for it until you were two blocks away and it was too far to go back so you put it on your head and kept going.

You got a job at a hotel restaurant that served breakfast to its guests as a part of their package deal. They arrived in waddling clusters between seven and eight every morning, meal vouchers in hand. The coffee was always too weak and the portions were too small. The toast was cold. They couldn't identify Canadian currency and left thirty-five cent tips. The waitresses had all worked there for years and rewarded themselves by proceeding directly to the hotel lounge after their shift and getting drunk before lunch. You joined them once, but felt ridiculous staggering back to the studio at one-thirty in the afternoon, a time you used to call *morning* not so long ago.

No matter. You were fired within the week for lateness.

There was a café across the street from the studio, and you got in the habit of meeting the twelve-year-old boy there after school. You bought the drinks, and he always ordered a three-dollar Italian soda. You reminded yourself of the free rent, and the fact that, in a curious way, he shielded you from the other intimidating café customers. Everyone there wore black, wrote in stained notebooks, rolled their own cigarettes. The employed ones splurged on vegan brownies, the unemployed ones did shifts outside, panhandling under the dripping awning until they earned enough to come back in again. There was one regular who you'd caught watching you. He was gaunt and looked twice your age and carried a guitar case that you'd never seen him open. His eyes were blue. You decided to come to the café by yourself soon.

That Saturday, you put the kettle on for the boy to make hot chocolate as he watched a rerun of *Friends* on the small black-and-white television. You told him you would return soon. He grunted assent, watching Jennifer Aniston.

The café was crowded, and the man was there. He waved you over to his table and you were grateful, because there was nowhere else to sit. Soon some French-Canadian kids joined you. They seemed to know the man, and laughed and complained that they had come here and had no money, no jobs and no prospects. You grew excited at the prospect of friends, and in a moment of reckless charity bought everyone at the table a coffee. Soon your packet of Drum and rolling papers were on the table, everyone helping themselves to thick pinches. Your guts felt hot, roiling from tobacco and espresso. A group of the French-Canadians went outside, and the man turned to you.

"So what do you do?" he asked. Embarrassed, you shrugged, wishing you had an answer.

"Nothing yet. A server, I guess. I haven't really—"

"I'm a poet," he interrupted. "I write poems about the government and multinationals and the things they do to screw over the people of this country. People like us."

You weren't sure if *us* included you but nodded as though you understood. He outlined the plan to publish his book, which he said would "blow the fucking lid off this shithole." The French-Canadians came back inside, and a girl whose name you were sure you heard correctly as *Pistou* plunked herself into the man's lap. They were all laughing and smiling, and you realized they'd gone out and got high. Your rolling papers were missing.

Pistou regarded you with a pout.

"Are you coming to the party?" she asked.

"Yes, there's a 'rave' tonight. You might enjoy it. It won't start for a few more hours though," said the man.

You remembered the boy and said you had to leave. The man loosened his grip on Pistou enough to slide a matchbook across the chipped mirror mosaic of the table.

"Write down your number," he said. "You and I have lots to discuss. You are special in the scheme of things, but you need to learn some stuff first. My poems will help you."

Unable to think of a reason not to, you wrote your friend's number on the matchbook and slid it back. As he pocketed it, Pistou snuggled in closer, floated you a lazy stoner wink, and laughed at a joke that existed only in her head.

The studio was filled with smoke. The kettle had boiled dry and the plastic handle caught on fire. The boy had gone out, left a note and forgot the stove. Your friend arrived home at the same time as the fire department. She was angry enough to want to throw you out, but she didn't. Left you there instead to clean the thick black smeary soot off the wall above the stove while she and her son went over to her boyfriend's house for the night.

You opened all the windows and scrubbed everything, but the smell lingered. It smelled like the winter of grade seven, when your mother bought your parka at a fire sale. She washed it three times, but you spent six months smelling wet smouldering wood and plastic every time you put it on.

It was after midnight when you finally collapsed on your air mattress, blankets taken from everyone else's bed to keep you warm with the windows still open. You couldn't sleep because of coffee and guilt, twisted the sheets into a useless rope. At 2:32 on your dollar-store travel clock, the phone rang. You rushed to it, imagined it was the fire department again, telling you you'd burned down something else. All you could hear on the other end was music and yelling. A party, a wrong number. You hung up and turned off the ringer. For nearly two hours the answering machine clicked on and off, capturing the same drunken, mildly aggressive message: "*Où sonts mes pantalons? Où sonts mes pantalons?*" Then laughter.

The next day, you called your mother. She agreed to wire you five hundred dollars, but wanted to make it clear that she considered this a failure on your part. You thought of asking her if it's possible to become so *good* at failing that it ceases to be failing. Much later, you wondered how she might have answered that.

You rolled up your air mattress for Vancouver, after having stayed on for two weeks past your original agreement. Your friend felt guilty, though you didn't know why. She cried at the ferry terminal, pressed a wrinkled twenty into your palm. Said she would miss you. The fire was forgiven now, and you smoked a joint with her before you boarded, just like the first time, and shared a laugh about that time as though it were ten years ago instead of a few weeks. Once aboard, you spent the entire twenty on magazines and the Pacific Buffet. A table all to yourself on a weekday afternoon. Plates full of mashed potatoes and roast beef covered in gravy. Stoplight-coloured Jell-O with caps of congealed whipped topping. You ate and read and kept your head down. In this fashion, time passed quickly.

In Vancouver, you got an apartment. Paid too much rent. Got and lost a succession of jobs in the service industry. Believed that the reason was not your chronic lateness or your inability to count cash, but the fact that you were too cerebral for such pursuits. Returned to school, and worked hard for the first time in your life. Fell in love. Found out you were wrong. Fell in love again, this time for real, and wondered how it was that you never saw it coming.

Now:

Tonight, walk down West Tenth Avenue when you're feeling sorry for yourself for any number of nebulous reasons. Look at the little Christmas lights on the houses and the sparkles they make on the wet leaves. Look at a bush with lovely white flowers, surprising this late in the fall. Someone has put a yellow post-it note on one of the leaves of the bush. She wants to know what kind of plant it is, because the flowers are so very beautiful and could someone please email her at fancypants@hotmail.com to tell her? Thanks!

Stand there for a spell, lingering over this bush and this post-it note. Keep the ink from smearing by catching the rain on the brim of your burgundy Kangol hat. Reach into your pocket and find a crumpled sandwich bag with Fig Newton crumbs in it and, admiring your resourcefulness, slip the bag over the branch and the post-it note.

Start walking again. Realize that finally, you are home.

Four-Letter Word for

Smells like Ovaltine, he thinks, pressing the collar of her coat to his face. He waits in her family's kitchen while she gets ready upstairs. It's a cheap cloth coat, faded and black, and too light, really, for winter. The edges of the sleeves are frayed and rubbed to a shine, and here smell more like smoke. He can see her standing on the corner at school, a cigarette in one unmittened hand. Smoke curling up over her fingers, into the tube of her sleeve, into the rough wool of her sweater. A cloud of breath behind the dark blinders of her hair.

He cannot yet attach a word to what he feels. There is a kind of tenderness, a need to caress which makes him think of animals, of fur. There is another need too, a yearning to hold her down in her stupid fairy-princess bedroom with those fluffy catalogue curtains her mother picked out. He needs to hold her down on that slippery lavender bedspread, make a man's voice in her ear. Everything in him constricts when he imagines her hot cheek against the satin sham.

He does not do these things. Instead, he returns her videos, walks her dog, helps her father with the crossword while she reads *People* on the chesterfield. She watches *21 Jump Street* reruns, and he memorizes the back of her neck. Saturday afternoons together in the rec room. She makes chaste dares: eat miniature marshmallows sandwiched between ketchup potato chips. Run through the snowy graveyard in sock feet.

He'll drive her to work at the SubStop tonight. She'll want him to close his eyes when he drives. Tell him which direction to turn the wheel. When to apply the gas. When to apply the brake. He hates doing it, but it's the only time he can make her laugh. She'll lean on the SubStop counter until eleven with her face in her homework, and he'll sit with her all shift. A free roast beef on white for him, and a Diet Sprite for herself. She can belch the alphabet straight through to "P."

He hears her on the landing, drapes the coat over a chair. He presses the heels of his hands against his eyelids until everything turns purple.

Farm Report

"Look at that," Shelly said, pointing at one of the trees. I expected to see a squirrel or a robin's nest. But I didn't see anything, and it looked to me like every other tree in the woods. I shrugged.

"There, dummy! Look—the tree has a *twat*." She grinned at me. I had never heard the word before, but I knew what it meant, especially when she walked over and poked at the niche in the bark with a stick.

Shelly Pinchak was my best friend. She was a year older than me but in my Grade 6 class. I think she had been held back in Grade 2 or 3. I was usually mean to the dumb kids, giggled when they had to read aloud, made fun of them on the playground, but Shelly acted smart in a way that had nothing to do with schoolwork. She used to live in the city.

Her family had moved into the old farmhouse down the road from us that had sat empty for several years. The last residents had been a lady truck driver and her no-good husband, the sort of people my mother didn't approve of. The first day Shelly had come over to play, my mother heard her say *ain't* and eyed her worn-out running shoes, her defiant chin and fierce cowlicks.

"They should just tear that old house down if that's the kind of people it attracts," she said after Shelly had gone home. We mostly played at her house after that.

Shelly had two tow-headed sisters, Tracy and Amy, both younger, and although I was an only child, the novelty of entertaining them soon wore off. They spent most of their time bickering over toys and television shows, so it wasn't difficult for Shelly and me to avoid them. Shelly's mom, Debbie, had gotten a job at the General Feed Mill, doing the books, and her dad, Gary, was a mechanic who wanted to "make a go" of farming.

"People've been doing it for thousands of years," he said, winking at me over their dinner table, "how hard can it be?"

He bobbed his shaggy head gently as he ate. I knew the answer to that question. I had seen parched crops and the bloated bellies of sick sheep—my father watching the *Farm Report* with his head in his hands. I thought it was best to be quiet and helped myself to another hotdog instead.

Shelly said her dad was a good mechanic, but most of the men on the farms already knew how to fix their own tractors and cars. Mr. Pinchak seemed to spend most of his time working on his own truck, feeding the geese, and building tire swings for "his girls." I liked being one of Mr. Pinchak's girls. My own father was always so busy with work. When I was little, Dad let me sit on his lap while he drove the tractor, teaching me to steer. We would walk back into the forest to watch the cattle drink at the pond, and when my legs got tired, he'd hoist me onto his shoulders. Then I got older and too big to be carried. I tried to tickle and hug him, and he'd place my arms back at my sides, saying, "You're too old for that now, go on with you." He looked as though he thought he might break me.

Shelly's dad didn't treat us like that. He gave us Superman rides—laying on his back in the grass, I balanced my hips on his big bare feet, his arms and legs stretched toward the sky. I clutched his oil-stained hands, afraid to fall, but Mr. Pinchak never dropped me.

"Easy does it, Supergirl, come on now," he said, and I would let go, one finger at a time, until I was flying.

I wanted to spend every moment at the Pinchaks' house.

Shelly came and went as she pleased, and every Saturday night Mr. and Mrs. Pinchak drove to the Legion to dance, and the girls didn't have to have a baby-sitter. We could do whatever we wanted then—dare each other to drink a glass of vinegar, smear peanut butter on our lips and try to get the dog to lick us, put uncooked spaghetti in a glass of hot tap water, and take it upstairs to her room, dip the still crunchy noodles in a saucer of ketchup, wave them around like cigarette holders before we ate them.

One night Shelly took my hand and led me on tiptoe into her parents' bedroom, dramatically pressing her finger to her lips. She opened the bottom drawer of their big old dresser. Under a couple of rumpled nylon nighties were stacks of *Playboy, Penthouse,* and *Playgirl*. Then she showed me the nightstand, where *The Joy of Sex* was, and a pile of mimeographed dirty jokes.

"My dad got these from work," she said. "I used to go to the garage on weekends sometimes, and they had some of them up on the walls. They had calendars with naked girls too." I leafed through the jokes, but I didn't understand what made them funny. We grabbed the book and a few magazines and took them back to her bedroom, pushing her dresser in front of the door. Shelly and I flipped through *The Joy of Sex*, lying beside each other, stomachs down on

Shelly's twin bed, with the book propped up on a pillow between us. My ears burned as we turned the pages, heat spiralling on a thick axis from my throat to my knees.

"I did that before," Shelly said, pointing to a drawing of a man with his hand between a lady's legs, "at my cousin's wedding."

"Where—on the dance floor?" I wasn't ready to believe her. Sometimes Shelly told me things just to see if she could trick me.

"Don't be a retard. It was my second cousin or something. I told him I was fourteen, and after we danced, we went out to the parking lot and got in the back seat of his car."

"Did you like him?"

"I think he was drunk, because his breath was terrible. And he kept pushing his tongue into my mouth, and it was really spitty and gross. The other stuff was okay though." She tapped the open page.

The lady in the picture had thick hair under her arms, something I had never seen before, and the man had a beard and long hair, like Mr. Pinchak.

May came, and with it my birthday, but Shelly was the star of my party. She won all the games, ate more cake than anyone, and even had the nerve to complain about the contents of her loot bag. She gave me the *Family Feud* board game.

I walked Shelly home after the party.

"When we play *Family Feud*, I'm going to be Richard Dawson," she told me. She grabbed me and kissed me hard on the cheek, the way the TV host did with the pretty girls on the show.

"Eww," I said, wiping my face with my forearm. "I don't think there's a Richard Dawson in the home game."

She reached into her blue Snoopy purse and pulled out a bottle. Tigress perfume, my favourite. Half-empty, I knew it was her mother's. She shrugged.

"I know you like it, so I took it from our bathroom." I imagined it on the back of the toilet tank, gathering dust. I rubbed the tiger-striped velvet bottle top with my thumb.

"Thank you," I muttered, certain that my mother would know I was using stolen perfume.

"Tigress," she whispered as she leaned into my ear, her chewed nails digging into my shoulder, holding me as we stood there on the side of the road, my left hand holding the contraband, my right resting lightly on her high, bony hip. We pretended we were sexy teenage runaways, hitch-hiking to the city, but no cars came.

❧

It was a hot day, the hottest spring on record, the radio man said, and the April sun dried us like raisins. The chicory and spit plants grew tall around our legs, whipping us with their thick stems. Shelly's cousin Kerry was visiting, and I hated her. She was almost as pushy as Shelly. She was prettier than both of us and knew it. It was Kerry who dared us to take off our clothes, so we did. We were all still as smooth as babies, but Kerry had breasts, not anything like my mosquito bites or Shelly's puffy nipples. She was showing them off, jumping around to make them bounce. As Kerry took off through the field, Shelly turned and winked. "What a *slut*," she whispered. I grabbed her hand, and we ran until we collapsed in the long grass, panting. When she kissed me, her mouth tasted like metal.

Shelly didn't enjoy bossing Tracy and Amy around, the way she did with me, but instead approached it as a kind of duty for the honour of being oldest. One afternoon, the girls had interrupted our checkers game with another downstairs yelling match. Shelly sighed and went down to the kitchen to administer threats. I sat in her room, waiting for her to come back, flipping the pages of her *Garfield* calendar. I went to her window to see what the geese were doing.

Mr. Pinchak had the pickup parked on the grass in the shade of the birch tree. He was shirtless, bent low over the open hood. I watched his arms work, ropey muscles twitching under tanned skin. On the dusty windowsill, a fat housefly, drunk with the heat, flung its logy body at the screen, trying to escape. Downstairs, I could hear Shelly shouting at her sisters in the kitchen, something about dinner and Mom and ice cream. Mr. Pinchak turned from the truck and looked at the house, shaking his head. Then he looked up and saw me at the window. I lifted my arm, to wave at him, but then my hand came down on my neck, and the other hand joined it, pushing my limp hair over one shoulder. Reaching behind my head, I undid the tie of my butterfly-print halter, letting the straps slip off, the whole shirt falling down to the top of my cutoffs. He opened his mouth like he was about to say something, looked at the kitchen window, looked down the driveway, then looked back up at me. I was holding my breath, my arms still half-bent and up by my shoulders. Goose bumps that felt like they might break my skin, my nipples tingling, itchy and hot. Then Mr. Pinchak—Gary—winked at me. I ran from the window, threw myself on Shelly's bed, and tried not to think. I looked at her Smurfette poster. *Anything boys can do, girls can do better*, it said. I ground my face into her stinky chenille bedspread.

I decided to stop watching cartoons in the afternoons. I started a new routine to match my new grownup feelings. Each day when I got home from school, I changed into play clothes, put my books away, grabbed a juice box, and kissed my mother on the way out the door.

"Where do you think you're going? You're spending far too much time over there, Allison. How anyone can stand having all those girls running around wild is beyond me . . ." she said, clucking her tongue.

"I'm not going over there," I said. "I just wanted to go for a walk back to the woods, Mom. Shelly got in trouble for something and can't come out anyways." I was becoming a much better liar.

"Hmm. Well, I'm not going to stand in the yard yelling for you half the night. Be home by six for dinner or else," she said.

"You bet, mummy mummer." But she had already turned her back to me and was cutting a chicken to pieces. I took my new route: through the field, once around the elm stump for good luck, a one-handed jump over the gate, and then across to the skeletal old barn behind the Pinchaks' house. Sometimes Mr. Pinchak was there, waiting for me, in our special place. There were crickets and ladybugs in the barn, empty rusted propane tanks, an old bilgy bathtub, an overturned wheelbarrow, and in the darkest corner, two sagging bales of hay. The sun shone through the holes in the roof, made the weeds grow, daubed the ground with green and yellow. This was where he brought me the first time, the afternoon Debbie and the girls had gone to visit their grandmother. That first day when we sat on the hay together, and he made jokes about how pretty I was and hugged me for a long time. So I stopped almost every day at the barn to see if he was there before I went up to the house.

Every time, he would ask me before he did anything, before he touched me anywhere. I liked the touching but hated having to give permission. I nodded my head a tiny bit, looking at my feet. Then the part when the talking stopped. I closed my eyes always, listening to his uneven breaths, my face pressed to his furry cheek like a teddy bear, so soft.

"You're a good girl," he'd say afterwards, stroking my hair, smoothing it down. The haziness in his eyes floated away like smoke, and he cleared his throat, becoming Mr. Pinchak again. "Now go and play, you. Okay?"

I didn't mind. It was so easy to be good.

Gary's thick black beard left a rug-burn rash all over me: my chin, shoulders, thighs. It thrilled me to lie to her, to have a secret tucked inside my pounding chest.

"I don't know, Mom . . . it doesn't itch or anything. Maybe it's that Avon bubble bath we got?"

"Well, we'll get rid of it then. And that—" she pointed at my bottle of Tigress on the dresser, "that diesel fuel will have to go too."

"Mom! No way!"

"Oh, yes way. Heaven knows what's in that stuff," she said. "Gives you a rash and smells ugly as sin."

School let out for the summer and I had big plans. In my imagination, I had already built a go-cart, explored the woods, and the Pinchaks had won the lottery and adopted me, and then we had all gone to Disneyworld to celebrate.

"We're moving again, you know," Shelly said one afternoon as I pushed her on the tire swing.

"How come? When?" My voice came out high and tight. Did Shelly know? Did anyone else know? I had heard people talk about girls "getting themselves in trouble," and was sure that's what I had done. Horrible images danced in my head. The faces of my parents, Mr. and Mrs. Pinchak, the flashing lights of police cars, the teachers and kids at school. I would have to move away, change my name. I would never see Mr.

Pinchak again. I stared at Shelly, tried to hear what she was saying.

". . . yeah, and Mom says she's had enough. She hates it here, she wants to go back to Burlington and get an apartment near Grandma."

"What about your dad?" I said, trying to sound uninterested.

"They had a big fight. She called him a bum. I dunno, they fought about this a lot, even before we got here. Mom thinks farms are dumb. I wanna go back too, this place smells like a toilet or something."

"When are you going?"

"I dunno . . . soon I guess. My friends in Burlington are way cooler anyways. Mom lets me ride my bike on the road and we all go down to 7-Eleven and hang out and drink Slurpees every day in the summer."

"Do you want to go upstairs and hang out now?" I asked, grabbing the rope of the swing, trying to stop it.

"Nah, not really. Besides, you just want to look at the naked ladies again. That's boring."

"I never said that! Let's do something else."

"You're weird, you know," Shelley said, spinning away from me. "You always want to do creepy stuff. Are you a sicko or what?"

I felt no relief. Shelly might not know, but somehow it

felt like everyone knew and had always known. An ugly stain that kept spreading, and everyone could see it but me.

The next weekend, as I watched from my yard, the Pinchaks' pickup pulled out of their driveway, followed by a U-Haul. I could see Shelly in the cab of the U-Haul as they drove past, sitting beside her dad. She didn't even look at me. She had barely spoken to me all week. Mom said it was because Shelly was sad, but I didn't believe her.

I rode my bike across the neighbours' lawns to the Pinchaks' house. I peered in the windows, cupping my hands around my face, saw the bare rooms, the dirty and worn linoleum. It was quiet in the yard without the geese honking and swaggering. The tire swing was still up, but I didn't sit on it. I walked toward the barn, kicking the gravel in the driveway, sending up little grey clouds of dust. I had gotten a splinter in my back the last time Gary and I had gone to the barn, and he had taken it out for me, his fingers working carefully while I winced and squirmed. With my back to him, he joked around while he pinched my skin, trying to distract me.

"Geez," he said, "three girls, but all tomboys . . . sure isn't the first time I've had to do this." He chuckled and then stopped.

"There you go, Allison," he said quietly. I turned around and he laid the splinter in my palm like a gift. It was jagged, grey and damp, the end tipped with blood.

I poked around in the dirt with my sandals, hoping that he'd left me something, some kind of souvenir, a valentine. I knew that he hadn't, but I kept looking anyway. Then I imagined him sitting on a bale in the corner, waiting for me. A grownup man sitting alone in the corner with his hands in his lap, waiting for a girl to cross the field. I laid down on the musty hay and breathed it in. The dust motes floated up into the shafts of sunlight. I bent my head down, let my hair fall over my face the way I did with Mr. Pinchak. I thought of the way certain things felt, and I hoped I could be a good girl again soon.

Good Tenants

My favourite thing about our apartment was the elm tree. Taller than our third-floor suite, its broad branches screened the hot late-afternoon sun, and its leaves made a comforting rustle outside the kitchen window. The apartment itself was fine too—Jim and I had moved in just before Andy was born, and there was a small separate room for a nursery. We could manage the rent, it was a clean building, and the other tenants were friendly enough. In those few sleepless weeks before the baby came, I'd get up in the middle of the night and watch Andy turn inside me: a pointy foot or elbow making a slow trajectory across my belly. Looking out the kitchen window, drinking an Ovaltine and watching the elm leaves shift in the breeze, I wondered what the rest of my life was going to be like.

The days I spent like any mother-to-be, sweeping the floors, straightening up, getting the nursery ready. Then Andy was born, and I had plenty to do besides dusting. Jim worked the day shift at the plant, so it was just me and the baby each day until suppertime. We spent a lot of time inside; the thought of washing and dressing us both, packing up bottles and diapers and stroller and handbag and getting out the door exhausted me before I even started. I felt safe in our apartment, and often the only interruption of my day was someone downstairs, using the old intercom system. At least once a week I would get someone who hit my buzzer by mistake.

"Miss Stanley?"

"No, next one up." I'd switch off before they had a chance to apologize.

Miss Stanley lived in the apartment above us. 4B. I was fairly certain I had never seen her. I knew the faces—and some of the names that matched them—on the third floor, but the top floor was a mystery. She didn't play loud music or have parties until all hours, but I figured, from the sounds I did hear, that she ran her business during the day. She mustn't have stayed up late, or maybe that was when she ran her errands. I imagined her piecing together makeshift dinners from the grocery store—cheese, bologna, a carton of gluey potato salad from the deli counter.

When Andy went for his afternoon nap, I would lie down in my bed as well. I could hear the sound of heels above me, and squeaking bedsprings.

The sounds of her creaky bed floated down through the ceiling. I could sometimes hear music in the rhythm of the squeaking. Usually the sounds started slow, like the first movements of a symphony, and then turned into a big number, heaving and rolling along like a show tune. I would let the sounds wash over me, forgetting everything else. I pictured her up there with her customers, first earnest and encouraging, and later all brisk business. Soft sounds she must feel obliged to make while she stared at the ceiling. *Does she think about the money while it's happening?* I wondered. *What do the men want her to do? Does she listen to them complain about their wives? Their bratty kids?* I had always imagined prostitutes as tough, carefree, and brave. Reckless streetwalkers, big-breasted gum-cracking girls. Shameless and smiling in pulled-up skirts and pulled-down panties, like the women in Jim's magazines. Was Miss Stanley much older than them? Her name conjured caricatures: a librarian in hair curlers, a secretary in a bathrobe the colour of sick. Maybe she was the wife these men never had.

The blind man's day was Wednesday. He always came up the street right around the time that Andy had his lunch.

I could usually tell which men on the street were going to be customers: nondescript portly men mostly, in waxy-looking suits or corduroy jackets. It was their quick, heads-down walk that gave them away. I watched them from the kitchen window, where I would hang out so far it was almost dangerous, smoking the cigarettes Jim thought I'd given up. On Wednesdays, the blind man came up the street with his head up straight. He was lanky, arms and legs looking a bit too long for his torso. His walk wasn't stiff but had a curious look of effort, like a man moving through water. He had a guide dog, and one day it stopped at the edge of the boulevard and shat. I watched as the blind man put a small plastic bag over his hand and knelt down, patting the ground to find it.

He never buzzed me by mistake, the way the others did. All those tiny round buttons squeezed so close together, but he had found the grace in his fingers to not make a mistake. I wondered if he was a good lover. Long fingers reaching out into the darkness, locating tiny places in the skin.

My husband reached for me every night, and most nights I spurned him. Jim was a tall man, and wide, with a big round head that made him look a bit like an overgrown baby. Andy had inherited this head, and the memory of his birth had not yet left me. Sometimes I felt like I had sacrificed my whole body for him. Looking in the mirror, I marvelled at how quickly my youth had vanished. My skin hung around my middle like a rumpled quilt. I stared at the slackening stranger who was now my reflection and felt betrayed.

When Jim touched me, I often pretended to be asleep, like a child. If he wanted to, he could have overpowered me, his pale, thick weight astride. Instead, he whined, which made the idea even less appealing. One night, his gentle but insistent rubbing of my back made me feel as though I were being sawed in half.

"The grocery money's in my handbag. Why don't you take it upstairs?" I whispered through clenched teeth. He slept on the couch that night and barely spoke to me for days.

One Wednesday afternoon, while Andy was asleep in his crib, damp bangs pasted to his broad, sweaty forehead, I snuck upstairs to the fourth floor. Turning left, I could see the door of 4B. The blind man's dog sat outside the door like a sentinel. A golden lab with his harness still on, he reminded me of the SPCA plaster donation dog at the mall. Was the dog not allowed inside Miss Stanley's apartment? Our building didn't allow pets, but certainly this was an exception. Maybe she was worried about the dog's smell, or it knocking things over with its burly tail. Maybe the blind man didn't want the dog to watch him.

That night, I took my husband's body into mine for the first time in months. I closed my eyes and he became the blind man, his bulk transforming into the blind man's long, lean frame. I ran my fingers down the length of his thin, imaginary arms. I guided his delicate hands to the places I needed them.

It got easier every time I imagined it, and it made him happy again. I knew I was being a good wife, at least on the outside. Jim started drying the dishes after dinner, pausing to kiss the back of my neck. He told me that the landlord said the elm tree might have to be cut down. "See those leaves?" he said. "At first, that just looks like all trees do at this time of year, changing, turning brown. But that's Dutch Elm all right. You wait and see, by next July, that tree will be deader than a doornail."

All through the summer and into the fall, I made Andy's lunch early on Wednesdays to make sure I had time to watch for the blind man. One day, as he became visible between the branches, I found myself wishing he could look up and notice me. I wanted to know his name, where he lived, what his life was like. What he and Miss Stanley did together. How much it cost.

The next Wednesday, he didn't appear. Andy sat at the table behind me, squeezing banana chunks in his chubby hands. *The blind man must be sick*, I thought, *or short of money, or fell and hurt himself.* Maybe he had simply rescheduled his visits. I was considering the possibilities when I turned around. Andy had managed to reach the sugar bowl on the kitchen table from his high chair and was licking a thick coating of sugar from his sticky banana fingers. I snatched the bowl from him and he let out a shriek. I smacked him hard across his fat face. His pink mouth opened wide. We stared at each other for a moment, like neither of us knew what to do next, and then he starting screaming again. A red patch in the shape of three fingers appeared on his cheek. I turned away to the window to light another cigarette, shaking with shame. Soon enough he stopped and went back to his sugary fingers, sniffling and snorting. *Let him eat the goddamn sugar,* I thought, *none of this is his fault anyway.*

The blind man didn't come the next Wednesday, either. I watched out the window for nearly an hour, stomach clenched. I was a week late for my period, and every cigarette I smoked was a hot stab of guilt. Andy had been sick with a fever, and was sleeping off the latest round of baby Tylenol. When I checked on him, he was snoring through his mucous. I tiptoed out of his room and found my cardigan.

Then I stepped out of the apartment and up the stairs to 4B. I knocked and waited.

She didn't even peek through the gap in the door with the chain on, just opened it. The air inside smelled like incense. Her apartment had the same layout as ours, from what I could see behind her. Something was boiling on the stove, fat plumes of steam winding up from the pot.

She looked a bit like my eldest sister. Her hair was fine and brown, and it frizzed out around her broad, handsome face. Her brows were much darker, pencilled in with precision. She wore a dressing gown that was silky and pink, but faded, and frayed around the hem. It had a print of scarabs on it. She looked a bit tired, but in a languorous, heavy-lidded way. I felt a sting of envy when I noticed the fullness of her breasts and her height—a good three inches taller than me. She was barefoot, her toenails unpainted.

"Yes?"

I realized that I hadn't figured out what to say, or even what exactly I was doing. I ought to have had a plan, a line of questioning. "Do you know . . . I mean, where . . ." *Where is he?* I wanted to say. *What have you done with him?*

"Is there something I can do for you?" she asked.

"Umm . . . no. Just, um, hello. I live downstairs and . . ." I looked down. "I thought I heard a strange noise."

"Hmm. Well, sometimes the pipes make a clunking sound. I was running a bath a while ago. Was that it?"

I tried on a neighbourly smile, found it didn't fit. "What I'm looking for isn't here."

"I'm sorry?" Her brows lifted.

"I really have to go," I said. "My son is downstairs. Sorry to bother you."

"Oh. Well, I'm sorry if I disturbed you . . . nice meeting you . . ."

I retreated down the hall. Around the corner at the top of the stairs, I stopped and tried to steady my breath. I heard her door close, then the quiet click of the deadbolt.

They started with the arms. The city workers began at the top and worked their way down, cutting branches of the elm into smaller pieces and dumping them into the big orange truck. They sliced the trunk into fat disks and loaded them in as well. I held Andy up to the window so he could watch. He loved the trucks and the sound of the chainsaws. Jim told me to look for black streaks inside the wood as a sign of the disease, but I couldn't see them from where we were.

"Looks like that promotion's pretty much sewn up," Jim said as we undressed for bed that night. "Might be foreman by this time next month." He put his arms around me, rested his warm hands on the small of my back. "That's more money, too. I was thinking, if this job comes through, we should think about getting a house. What do you think? Get you some more trees?"

He moved his hands up to my shoulders, holding me out in front of him so he could see my face. I thought of the baby inside me, a bungalow with no floors above me, of Andy playing in the yard under a maple. And navigating a new house at night, fingertips brushing along the walls in the darkness.

I took his beefy face in my hands.

"Close your eyes," I whispered before I kissed him.

Runa

I got this tattoo on my ankle, says "runa." People ask me what it means sometimes, and I usually make somethin' up, tell them it was the name of a friend or some shit, cuz the truth's embarrassing, you know? I was thirteen, maybe fourteen. I thought I was pretty hot shit back then, oh yeah. So this one time I'm crashed at DeeDee's place for a few days. Nice broad, made me dinner—the whole bit. First I thought she must want to sleep with me or something, you know? Cuz who gives a kid a place to crash for nothing? People always wanna get something if they can. But she was pretty cool. Turned out she had worked the street too.

So anyway, she tells me she knows how to do these homemade tattoos, and do I want one? I figure, sure why not?

Plus I won't have to pay for it. She heats up this thing she made outta an old pen and a needle, over the stove flame, you know? We both take a few slugs of Southern Comfort, then she goes to work on me. Holy shit, did it hurt! I was cryin and wavin my arms around and shit, and finally she gets right pissed at me, says she's gonna stop if I don't smarten up. I tell her, okay, whatever, fuckin stop cuz I'm dying. My whole fuckin leg's on fire, feels like. That's why she only got halfway done writing "runaway."

Letters from the Pink Room

I have to take the SkyTrain and then a bus to get to my job. The office is tucked into the corner of a half-vacant strip mall. It has tinted windows and a locked glass door with the words *Studio Entertainment* in small peeling letters. Inside, the walls are bluish-purple and the carpet is dark, short, industrial.

There's a narrow hallway with three doors on each side. The walls have cheesy murals painted on them between each doorway. Chinese ladies, tigers, lush forests. I assume that the murals are to cover up the one-way mirrors in the rooms, but I don't know why those were ever there.

Down the hallway, off to the right, is the bathroom and shower, and the kitchen/lounge/laundry room. There's a microwave, sink, fridge, coffeemaker, washer/dryer, couch, and laundry hamper. You could live in here if you really wanted to, but there aren't any windows back here.

The rooms are colour-coded: the cherry room, the rose room, the green room, the blue room, the purple room, and the pink room. The pink room is my favourite because it makes my skin look the nicest, and the little cassette player actually works. It's become my "lucky" room too. I think because it's often Clarissa's room, and she's our big money-maker. She has lots of stuff in bags under the bed. Once I borrowed some shoes for my show without asking.

I put my knapsack in my room and get some sheets and pillowcases, fresh from the dryer. The beds are futon mattresses on sturdy wood frames. The mattress and the pillowcases have crinkly white plastic covers on them, like in a hospital. I always the choose burgundy sheets from the laundry room, because of the skin thing again, and because they match the room colour the best.

I make my bed and get changed into whatever outfit I'm going to wear, usually a tank top and panties, although sometimes I wear a PVC corset or garter belt and stockings. It just depends on how much energy I have: the wilder my outfit, the more likely I am to have to entertain the fetish guys. And that can be tiring. I always wear a wig though; a platinum blonde one, with bangs. I put on more makeup: shimmery lotion all over, sparkly eye shadow, dark liner all around my eyes to make them stand out, lip liner, and tons of gloss—a sticky mess in real life, but it looks just right on video.

I log in then, set up my camera and check my sound levels. I usually go pee, get some water or a coffee, and then I start working.

Before I started this job, I told my boyfriend, Bryan. As a regular consumer of all things pornographic, he was aroused. At the same time, Bry hated the thought of other men masturbating while looking at me, and him not being included in the fun. The only other person that knew about my job was my friend Mark. I trusted him, and it made me feel safe to see his curiosity tinged with paternal disapproval. It also turned me on.

I told myself (and Bryan) that I would have to make serious coin, like a hundred bucks an hour, to do "something like this." I assumed that I would be raking it in, but obviously make less than a stripper or a prostitute, who have much closer contact with their customers. But just like those girls, I only make money while I'm working, not while I'm standing around waiting for customers. There's no time clock or punch cards, no benefits or sick days. If I don't show up for a shift and don't call in ahead of time, I get charged a fifty-dollar fee for the unused room. Still, I figured my stint in "the industry" would at least pay the bills.

My friend Beth had answered an ad in the *Vancouver Sun*. Her temping job at the bank didn't work out, and she was desperate for cash. I saw her on the SkyTrain on the way to her interview. She was all dressed up, the way anyone would for an interview, but with a little more makeup, a bit more cleavage than would usually be appropriate. I asked her to let me know how it went, that I might be interested too. She promised she would call, and a few days later, she did.

Beth hadn't been working there long, but she told me she expected to be making good money soon. "It's all about getting regulars," she told me. "Once you've got regulars they come all the time and stay on forever. Plus, I guess they tell their friends or something. Also, the more people go to your site, the more hits you get, people get curious, new guys come and check you out just to see what all the hits are about."

It made sense. I would be able to work nights, which was a plus. With my part-time job at the mall, four courses at the college, and my work-study position, I didn't have any daytime left over. I might be able to do my homework in the slow times. I could stay at school until nine or so, go in and work a 10 P.M. to 4 A.M. shift, then sleep in the room until the morning shift came in, have a quick shower and head back to campus. I liked the idea of it. The drama, the tragic glamour of dirty underwear and cigarettes and coffee and my new secret life.

Kyla's the manager, and she's the one who interviews me. She's a big girl. Tall and heavy, with long curly brown hair and a friendly, small-town face. She looks like a woman who pours the draft at a low-rent sports bar, or rings groceries through at the corner store. Her office is small, but there's a loveseat beside her desk. She clears off some stacks of papers and books to make room for me to sit. She has pictures of black men, fashion models pinned to her bulletin board. She tells me she likes black guys. I ask her about the job.

"Well, most girls work in the 'Girls Home Alone' room, but there's other rooms too, like 'Fetish' and stuff. Mostly you'll start off in 'Girls Home Alone,' but go ahead and set up your second terminal in 'Fetish' if you like. The guys aren't bad, but don't go near the 'Dungeon' room, and if you do, charge, like, six bucks a minute and get ready for freaks. I never work there."

"Okay." I try to imagine what kinds of things "freaks" might want to do.

"Most of the customers are really nice. I have lots of regulars, and they're total sweeties, y'know? Sending me emails and poems, pictures, real sweet guys."

"Wow," I say, but I'm thinking, *sounds like a bunch of losers*. I didn't come here to make new friends.

"Yeah, you'd be surprised. If anyone comes on and you don't wanna do something or he says anything about animals or incest or anything you just block his IP number and then he can't come back on. Plus, that shit's illegal, so he'll get a nasty message from head office. The chat rooms are all monitored, but just the free chat, where anyone can read it. Don't worry, no one at head office is looking at your live video show!"

Yeah, right. If I worked at head office and could spy on people, I know I would. But at least they're protecting me from the weirdos.

"So what exactly do I have to do?"

"Well, most guys just want the basics, y'know, show me yer boobs and all the rest and they do their thing and that's it. But whatever you want to do beyond that is cool. Guys can also call the phone in the room and talk on the phone with you while they're watching you at their computer at home. Lots of guys really like that, that they can see you talking right to them. But yeah, whatever, y'know? Dress up, play mistress or whatever. Some of the girls are produce-friendly too, so yeah, that's always good. Bring any toys or sexy stuff you got at home, and have just fun with it. We've had some girls here for years. This is the only work they do, and they're making thousands. Wait and see, it's really fun. Now let's pick your screen names . . ."

Because I work two terminals at once, I need to use two different names to maximize my money-making potential. We look at the list of names currently in use, to get ideas, and to avoid repeats. Any name that has *hot, tits*, or *sexy* in it seems to be taken. Kyla asks me about nicknames, former pets, and sexual preferences to help me decide. We finally settle on *1foxylady* and *kissme*. Kyla shows me how to log in, how to take archive pictures that customers can look at while they're browsing, how to type my daily message:

****SUPER HOT BLONDE KITTEN FOR YOU!!!*** BRAND NEW NAUGHTY SLUT, LOVES TO FUCK AND SUCK YOUR COCK!!****SWEET AND PRETTY, BIG BOOBS AND A TIGHT ASS...CUM AND PLAY WITH ME!!! ***T1 SERVER***ZOOM***AUDIO***PHONE***

I hate typing in all uppercase letters and using multiple exclamation points, but it looks like I might be the only Girl Home Alone who doesn't make any spelling mistakes. I ask myself if that means I shouldn't be here at all.

It's tricky at first. Each room has two computer terminals in it, one for each of my screen names. Each monitor displays my "free chat," where me and my potential customers can type messages to each other. They can't see me yet, but they can look at my archived pictures to check me out. Between the two computers and no limit to how many people can be on the free chat with me at once, it can be confusing. I sit on the edge of the bed, looking from the left screen to the right screen, trying to be perky and sexy and not get confused as I shift from keyboard to keyboard. Then, if a customer decides to log in to either of the paid rooms, the camera sends my live image to the customer. I know when someone logs on because a little icon appears on one of my monitors and the computer makes a *ka-ching* sound, like a cash register. If they have a sound card, they can hear me too. I usually abandon the free chat on both terminals at this point. Sometimes the other free chat customers know what's going on, and one of them will log on to the other computer just to watch.

Then there's the phone. Customers can call me on the phone in my room and talk to me while they watch me on screen. I like this because it makes my job a lot easier. Without the phone, they can hear me, but I can't hear them, which means they're still typing what they want me to do on the screen. It's very hard to read from back there on the bed, especially without my glasses on.

What's funny is, that after the first couple of weeks, it's just like any other job. I can even email my friends from work, although Mark asks me to stop, because he says it makes him uncomfortable. He tells me this when we're out for a drink, and I'm imagining that he loves me. Bryan just teases me about my slutty-sounding message of the day. Sometimes he comes into one of my free chat rooms and tries to trick me by pretending he's someone else. I usually figure it out fairly quickly.

I go in, I have good nights and bad nights, I take breaks, I go home. Same old thing. I'm starting to care more about the money though, now that I know how to work the terminals and I'm less nervous.

I feel a bit like a McDonald's drive-thru. You know when you're really hungry, and you want something real and nourishing and good, but you can't have that—maybe it's late or you don't want to cook or you don't have any food at home. Fast food is the only choice you've got, so you take it, and for the first few bites it's really good, it's just what you wanted, even though you know it's bad for you and you're going to feel like a bag of crap later on? Yep, that's me. The Big Mac of virtual sex.

I get paid in cash every week. The per-minute rate that I charge my customers gets cut three ways. First, head office gets half. The remaining half is split between the office and me. That means if I work for ten minutes, at three dollars a minute, the customer gets billed for thirty dollars. I get $7.50.

It makes me feel good sometimes, to provide this service. It's not hard work, and I'm able to reduce myself to the lowest common denominator. Tits and ass, that's what I'm made of and what the hell is wrong with that? I don't have anything to be ashamed of, and besides, sometimes it is fun, sometimes I even come. I laugh with the nice old married men on the phone, or the sweet nerdy student in Florida. And then this guy from New York calls and he sounds like Barry White, and I mean *exactly* like Barry White, and I'm trying not to laugh, and then he starts calling me a bitch and a slut and making me say these things back to him, so I'm rolling around on the bed, with the camera remote beside me to zoom in and the phone in my hand, and saying, *yeah, I'm such a dirty fucking slut, I'm such a stupid bitch-cunt-whore*, and he's making me fuck my own asshole and it hurts like hell and I really want to stop but I can't because of the money, so then I start thinking about the money and getting it over with quick, but not too quick because the longer I can stand this, the more stupid goddamn money I'll make and all of a sudden it isn't any fun at all. And every name that Barry White calls me is true.

Today I took some new archive shots with the remote camera. The more free pictures I have posted for potential customers to peruse, the better. I don't do anything too nasty, like some of the girls; I think it's better to be a tease so that the customer will want to pay for it. So it's mostly just shots of my bum in panties or my cleavage. But today I took one of me sucking my fingers. I looked at this picture of me with two fingers in my mouth, looking all sidelong and hungry, long blonde wig hanging down. I look like a porn star. It surprises me, how much I can replicate this look, this artificial sexy lady routine. I look like the sort of girl who likes to suck cock for a living. Needless to say, it is my best picture of the day. And business is good.

I'm not making a dime tonight. It's just me and Marjorie working the late shift. I sit around, try to do some homework, but I have to keep looking up at the terminals to see if anyone logs on. The usual bunch pass through the free chat—teenagers and other goofs, looking for some free dirty talk—but hours pass without a single paying customer. These are the bad times, coming in here for nothing, losing sleep, when I could be at home in my bed.

I put the *Gone to pee, back in a sec!* sign in front of the my camera and leave the lights on. I make some coffee and take a cup to Marjorie.

Marjorie is pretty old for this line of work. She has these faded, runny-looking blue tattoos all over her arms and wrists, but I hear she does all right. She's been here for a double-shift today: sixteen hours. Her smell fills up the room and makes me nervous. Do I smell like that too?

It reminds me of my job at the lingerie store in the mall, when I go into the tiny changeroom with some lady in her panties, to help her adjust a bra or fasten a corset, smelling that private, under-the-clothes smell, that woman smell, feeling like I'm privy to a secret. Marjorie does not have a good-smelling secret. Later, when I go back to the kitchen to turn off the coffeepot and empty the grounds, I see Marjorie's carrot in the garbage can. I put the lid down quick and go for a long break.

That night I sleep there for the last time. The heat is always on in the rooms, so we don't get cold when we're naked, but it makes it hard to sleep. I set the alarm on my watch, hoping it's enough to wake me. The band digs into my wrist. The droning sound of the still-on equipment and the blue lights coming off the monitors and the sweaty feeling of the crinkly plastic undersheet make me restless. I think about the real men, the ones I care about, and the men who mean nothing. I think about how easy it is to get them mixed up, to coo and wiggle my way through conversations outside of this room, and then expect some kind of caring from a man on the other end of the phone. I dream of hospital beds and people dying.

Bryan can't stand it anymore. He hates my job and he wants me to quit. I tell him it's because he's too close to the action now, that I've gone and spoiled the detachment that makes porn so interesting. He says it's because he loves me. I feel empty, but I put on a good show. I even cry.

So this is how it ends. I dump Bryan by email, and he replies that he's been expecting it. I am in Mark's bed the next day. I tell Mark that I don't want to go back to work ever again, and this pleases him. I phone Kyla from his apartment and tell her I won't be coming in anymore, and that Beth will pick up my last pay envelope for me. As I'm getting out of Mark's shower, he sings along with The Police CD he's put on. *Roxanne, you don't have to turn on the red light*, he serenades me in my towel, and I laugh. How easily he's rescued me. None of this will last, of course, but for the time being he is my hero, the only one who knows me, knows this story. I will tell it a hundred times after Mark is gone, to a hundred more men, and every time it will be different. No one gets the whole picture; they only get what they need. They will all fall in love with me. I know just what to say to men.

Up-Island

I'm standing at the sink, rinsing out my mug, and I hear the school bus before I see it. I look up and there it is, past the big window behind me and reflected back in the window over the sink. The double reflection makes a loud orange smear on the early winter twilight. Then there's a loud double-honk.

It's got to be Runa.

I wasn't expecting her; she's never come down to visit me before. I hope the next-door neighbours don't freak out about having a school bus parked outside. They don't own the four-plex any more than I do, but you'd think they did, the way they're always farting around in the garden and bitching when I leave my ashtray out on the porch. I go stand in the doorway as Runa parks the bus beside the fence. She leaps out and stomps up the walkway, arms outstretched. "Wendy!" she bellows, and I'm about to say something hostess-y, like *what a nice surprise*, when I see the black eye. She hugs me so hard something pops in my back. We go inside and I stash the Hemp-Plus granola in the cupboard and get her a Coke.

Runa tells me she left Mike this afternoon—threw some stuff in the bus while he was out at the Cold Beer and Wine, then drove straight down to Victoria from Comox. She's decided she wants to go downtown tomorrow and file a report with the police. "But first, I thought I'd come and get a little moral support," she says, helping herself to my cigarettes.

"Shouldn't you have gone to the cop-shop back home?" I ask.

"Fuck that shit," she exhales.

I've been living in this place for about three months now, since the beginning of October. When I first got into town, I lived in this shitty basement apartment for a month. I had a futon, but no frame for it, and after a few weeks of it sitting on the basement floor, the whole thing grew mildew on the bottom, and now I have to put an extra sheet on it so it doesn't smell so bad.

I give Runa the grand tour, tell her about my nosy neighbours.

"So one morning, I made my breakfast, and then afterwards, I'm sitting on the porch having a smoke, and Peggy comes out and she's all 'We smelled bacon frying!' and I'm like, what does this woman want me to say?"

"You should have told her to fuck off and mind her own business."

"Yeah, so then she starts telling me how they really noticed the smell because they don't eat bacon anymore because of the nitrates or something and it's so bad for you, so finally I just have to butt my smoke and go inside and close the door in her face or she's going to stand there yapping about her and her boyfriend all frickin' day."

"Oh, man, I say we eat nothing but BLTs the whole time I'm here!" She yells "BLTs" loud.

Runa is a waitress at Lee's Pagoda, the Chinese place in Comox. She serves oily chow mein and Singapore Slings to a steady clientele of mostly locals. "Eat at Lee's, have greasy pees!" is Runa's favourite joke, said in a horrible fake-Chinese accent like Benny Hill. She does all right for tips, since she's friendly and knows nearly everyone in town. She told me that she saves some of her tip change in one of Mike's old work socks. "I worry that he'll find it, so I keep moving the hiding place. Some day you and I will have enough money saved up to finally fly to L.A. and party with our rock 'n' roll boyfriends."

It's something we planned back in Grade 11, that someday we'd pack up and move to Los Angeles. We'd go to the clubs and party every night, and everyone would talk about "those wild Canadian chicks." Eventually, I'd end up marrying Axl Rose and she'd marry Tommy Lee and we'd live happily ever after. At the time, it sounded possible, even likely. I'm embarrassed by it now, obviously, but what's more embarrassing is that Runa still clings to it like it's something real, something just around the corner for both of us.

I owe Runa a lot. She was the one who scored us the killer seats for Guns N' Roses. She was the one who took me to the emergency room when I got that horrible itching and thought I had a disease, and it was only a yeast infection. She drove me all the way to Nanaimo once, on the spur of the moment, just because I said I felt like going to Burger King. She didn't get mad when I left that home highlighting kit on her way too long and bleached most of her hair white as snow. But now that I live here in Victoria, things are different. I'm trying really hard to fit in here and make some new friends. So far, it hasn't been that successful. People are polite and everything, but maybe I just need to give it some more time. All I know is, none of those people would even *talk* to me if they knew I had a Mötley Crüe poster in my bedroom—so I hid it in my closet, along with some of my CDs and T-shirts. I don't tell Runa this though; she still thinks we're sharing the same high-school crushes on guys in metal bands. Besides, now that she's sitting in my living room, I'm glad she's here. It seems stupid to worry about what other people think of her.

"Hey, come check out the bus!" she says, grabbing my arm. Runa's had the school bus for ages. One good crop of Mike's homegrown financed its purchase, and while the grow-op is long gone, the bus is still her baby. The outside still mostly looks like a school bus, except for a section on the rear driver's side that she started painting a mural on about two years ago. It's black primer with faded yellow stars. The interior is what she works on lately, but it always looks the same to me: a kind of giant rolling toolshed. An old mattress reclines limply on a raised platform in the back, and a vinyl-topped card table is bracketed to the side wall. The rest of the space is littered with cardboard boxes and tools, folding chairs and old sweaters, pieces of lumber. You have to watch out for nails on the floor.

This time though, she *has* done a bit of work: the wall opposite the card table has some tongue-in-groove paneling up, and onto that, she's thumb-tacked some black-and-white pictures. They're photos of Runa, taken by a girlfriend of hers, Sandy, who I've never heard of. I surprise myself by feeling a bit jealous. They're *artistic* shots, mostly taken outside—Runa naked and draped with a sheet, Runa rolling around on the grass, Runa perched in a tree. Runa's not exactly your artistic-naked-lady type. In most of them, she's still got her rocker boots on. She's not fat, but she's no ballerina. She's proud of the photos though.

"So who's Sandy?" I ask.

"She's Timber's new girlfriend. She's really cool and fuckin' wild, man. She's got a ring in her clit!"

"Yeah, sure she does."

"I'm serious, Wendy. She showed me in the bathroom at Deb's house."

I don't want to hear any more about it, so I kneel down to look closer at the pictures.

"Has Mike seen these?"

"Hell, yeah," she says. "He fuckin' loves them. I made sure that Sandy hung on to the negatives though. I don't want him doing anything stupid. I thought it might be weird, y'know, letting somebody else see me naked, but I guess with other chicks it's all right. I think it turns him on."

She tells me that Mike's still on his medical EI, on account of the time he buggered up his back falling off the roof on the job site. I wonder if he didn't *jump* off—from the sounds of it, he's been milking it for months. From how Runa tells it, he's always playing the Xbox his co-workers chipped in for, and draws comic-book ladies, smokes pot, and makes excuses for not doing his physio exercises.

Mike and I went out for a while, in Grade 10. My friend Roxanne had just broken up with him and told me he was bad news, but considering some of the creeps we were hanging out with at the time, I didn't pay much attention. Mike was a few years older than me, owned his own car, always had weed and beer (or at least the money to get them), and he said I was pretty. He also liked to draw, and for a while, I imagined romantic scenes of reclining nude on the duct-taped sofa in his parents' basement while he sketched me.

We had only been seeing each other a couple weeks when he gave me a ring. I was touched by the gesture but worried I was most likely wearing something stolen. Things got deeply weird after that. He tried to keep me from hanging out with my other friends and was always calling my house late at night to see if I was actually home in bed and not out with somebody else. Even my parents were starting to notice that something was up. I tried to dump him, but he kept calling and leaving roses and drawings on my porch. He called early one Sunday morning, and my dad answered the phone, and lost it on him: threatened to call the cops or kick his ass if he didn't take the hint. A few weeks later, he was dating Runa. I warned her, but it worked even less than Roxanne warning me. Besides, she had seen it all anyway and that didn't seem to scare her off. My feelings weren't hurt that much—unless you plan to break the mould and run off with the French teacher, the small-town dating pool is pretty limited.

I still hung around with Runa, because she was my best friend, but I tried to avoid Mike when I could. It's never been easy because he pulls the same shit with her as he did with me, but worse. And now there's this black eye, which isn't the first bruise he's given her.

"It's not like I haven't tried to end it with him," she says, pushing some clothes off a chair for me to sit down. "Last time I tried to leave, the cops found him on a side road with a goddamn tube stuck on the tailpipe of the truck, the other end in the window, and the engine going. Stupid bastard was going to kill himself. For *me!*" she says. The look on her face is wistful and romantic, as though he'd written her a poem. Too bad he didn't have a proper garage, I think.

Runa and I walk down to the liquor store together before it closes and get a bunch of wine coolers. I don't drink wine coolers anymore, but I still do when I'm with

Runa, because she's never liked the taste of beer. After the liquor store, we swing by the KFC to pick up a bucket of chicken and some macaroni salad for dinner. The pimply kid behind the counter is staring at Runa so much he can barely take our order. She's not looking her foxiest, in her faded pink Club Monaco sweatshirt and no coat, but her shiner is impressive. These tarted-up blonde girls who're waiting for their order are totally gawking too. Runa can't resist. "You think I look beat up? You should see the *other* chick!" she snorts. The blondes back up like she's going to kill them. Luckily, acne boy returns with their order, and they're out the door.

I know that I've only been out of Comox for a few months, but it seems like forever sometimes. Runa's the only part that I imagine myself holding on to. But when I see her, and I know it isn't fair, she just reminds me of all the things I hated about home. I guess it wouldn't be so bad if I went up there to see her, but having her come down here is like having to deal with a drunk relative who might embarrass you at any moment. I know how relieved I'll feel when she's gone.

Runa may not have packed much in the way of clothes, but she was organized enough to bring her old VHS copy of Metallica's *Cliff 'em All* and the classic purple bong with her. I gather up some paper towels and a couple forks, and

I'm getting settled down on the couch when Runa says, "What're you doing?"

"What?"

"Don't you wanna come and party in the bus?"

"But there's no TV in there."

"So bring yours out."

I've got one of those cheap TV/VCR combo units from the drugstore, so it's not a big deal, until we have to spend the next twenty minutes hunting up extension cords to string together to make it out to the bus. It's a good thing I didn't smoke any weed first.

I've almost got the whole thing joined together, a long snake of cords running from the backyard outlet over the fence, and Runa's in the bus setting the TV up on the card table, when Peggy comes around the side walkway.

"Oh, hi, Wendy," she says, like she was just passing through and is surprised to find me here.

"Hey, Peggy." I pretend to be fascinated with the cords.

"That sure is a long string of cords you're making. Are you going to be using some power tools?"

Is she retarded? "Nope, we're just going to watch some television in my friend's bus," I reply. *Why am I even bothering to tell her anything?*

"I see . . ." she trails off, looking at the bus. "Is your friend from out of town?"

I totally see where this is going. "Just up-island. And no, she won't be staying long."

"Oh, I wasn't thinking that," says Peggy. "I was just concerned about the parking bylaws and whatnot. I wouldn't want your little friend to get in trouble with the municipality or anything."

God, I want to wring her neck.

Then Runa flings wide the door of the bus and proclaims, "Let us commence with the motherfucking rock and roll!" and Peggy actually lifts her hands up for a second, like something's being thrown at her.

"Well, I won't keep you," she says to me. "I was just wondering, Wendy, if I leave you some money, would you be able to bring me a pound of Sumatra home from the shop? We're nearly out, but I'm in meetings all day tomorrow and don't have time to go shopping."

Runa scowls as she walks over to the fence and grabs the end of the cord-snake. "Hey, are you trying to buy weed off my friend here?"

"Weed? I don't know what . . . oh no! I'm asking her to bring me some coffee. Coffee from her work."

I shiver. I can see Runa looking over at me.

"Tomorrow's Tuesday though. She has to go to school."

"School? I don't think that Wendy goes to school, do you dear? She works nearly full time at The Beanery, isn't that right? Or am I wrong?" she says, swiveling her small, pert head back and forth between us.

"I'm just going to go hook this up now. Goodnight, Peggy," I say finally, and step into the bus, leaving their two confused faces in the growing dark.

We don't say much to each other until we get settled in, the tape's playing and we're eating chicken on the bed.

"So are you going to tell me what the hell's going on?" asks Runa, as she twists the top off her cooler.

"Honestly, Runa, it's so not a big deal. I'm just working full-time right now, that's all."

"Oh, come on, Wendy. You move away and tell everyone you're going to school and then you hardly ever call me. And I saw Nick the other day and he told me that you haven't called Tracy once, in like, the four months you've been here. And now your fucking neighbour tells me that you aren't even in school. What the fuck, man?"

"But I did come here to go to school, honestly."

"Then why aren't you there? Why are you acting so weird?"

"Because, goddamn it . . " I'm trying to get a piece of macaroni to slide onto the tine of my fork. "Because I didn't get in, okay?"

The problem with not getting into school was that I never actually applied. After I graduated from high school, I just kinda coasted around Comox for a couple years. It didn't take long before I was sick of living in shitbox apartments with immature assholes and working the checkout at Pro Hardware. I started thinking that maybe I should go back to school—I could go to college and do the Dental Assistant program, or even apply as a mature student at the University of Victoria—my high-school grades were pretty good, considering how little I showed up, so why not? When I was a kid, I always wanted to be a veterinarian. Maybe I still could. University seemed like such a good idea, and I even got as far as telling people that I was going. I had all the pamphlets and the forms, but when it came time to fill them out and send them in, I just felt so stupid. I kept looking at all the stuff I had to fill out and thinking about getting a student loan, and every time I sat down to deal with it, I just seized up somehow. Then the phone would ring or it would be time to go to work and I'd put it off for another day. All this time, I was still telling people that I was moving to Victoria at the end of August. Then summer was nearly over and it seemed easier to just go than to tell the truth. It's not like anybody made a big deal out of it.

My parents didn't even give me a going-away present or

anything. I think they were glad that I was going back to school, because they want me to do well and all that crap. I know they care about me, it's just that they're always busy with other stuff, mostly my overachieving brother and sister. I've always just done my own thing anyway, and I think Mom and Dad were glad to have me in the middle. I gave them a bit of a rest. My dad used to refer to me as "the kid he didn't have to drive anywhere."

The weekend before I left, I had a little dinner party at Lee's with Runa, Nick, Tracy, and a couple other people, but that was it. I came down here and got a job and an apartment. I'm not lonely exactly. I'm surrounded by people all day at my work. But my parents think I'm at school, so I call them once every couple of weeks and tell them that everything's fine, and I haven't really kept in touch with anyone else. Except Runa.

And I guess this sounds fucked-up, but in a weird way, Runa's pretty lucky. Sure, her life sucks in lots of ways, but whose doesn't? And she's got a lot of good stuff going on too: friends, a steady job she likes, a house. It's not perfect, but it's more than a lot of people have.

I try to explain this all to Runa, except for the part about not actually applying, and the part about her being lucky, but it comes out sounding stupid.

"I'm working lots and saving up, so I'll just reapply next year, and everything will be fine. Runa, come on; don't look at me like that. I didn't want to be one of those people that talks all the time about getting out of town and then never does. I hate that crap."

Runa shakes her head and starts rooting around in the chicken bucket. "Why didn't you tell me?"

"Because I was embarrassed."

"That's bullshit, man. We tell each other everything—or at least we used to. What the fuck?"

"I don't know. I guess I just wanted to have a secret."

"A secret?"

"Yeah, it's like, everyone back home knows every single thing about me, and I was sick of it. It's like, if I went away for a while, maybe that could change, and maybe I could change too. So when I fucked up, there was no way I was going to bail on moving, but I wasn't going to tell everyone the truth either."

"Did you think we would have cared that you didn't get in? God, don't be so paranoid—"

"No, it's not even about that. Even though it was totally retarded and even though it doesn't make any sense, I wanted it to be a secret. It would be something that was mine, something that didn't belong to anybody else for a change. Here, I don't have to tell anyone anything. I feel . . . alone. But safer, if that makes any sense."

"Not really."

"Here—have the last drumstick."

After my going-away dinner at Lee's Pagoda, Nick and Tracy bailed, so me and Runa went back to her and Mike's place to drink some more. After an hour or so, Mike came home and you could tell he'd probably been out drinking his cheque at the peeler bar all day with his buddies. Runa and I were listening to the B-52's and singing along and laughing and jumping up and down on the couch. When he saw what a good time we were having, he got all pissy and starting whining about how an injured man couldn't get any peace and quiet even in his own goddamn house. We kept goofing around, ignoring him. I was laughing harder than I felt inside. Runa took a breather to go to the washroom, and I collapsed on the couch. Mike watched her go, and then swiveled the recliner towards me. "You two are pretty cute together, you know that?" he said. "Are you thinking what I'm thinking?" He rubbed his open palms on his thighs.

"Jesus Christ, I hope not. And if I am, then you're gross."

"Oh, come on," he said with a beery grin. "I know how chicks get after a few drinks, falling all over each other."

My legs were wobbly and tired from all the jumping. I felt a bit dizzy too. "Yeah, well, that doesn't mean anything. Maybe women are just more comfortable being affectionate."

He leaned forward. "Oh, yeah, I remember how affectionate *you* were. Remember, Wendy? You fuckin' loved it, didn't you?"

"God, Mike, why do you have to be such an dork? We broke up, like, four years ago. Get a grip."

"Awww, c'mon, Wendy. Those were some good times we had. Why can't you be nicer to me? You're nice to every other guy in town. At least that's what I hear."

"Shut up, Mike." But I said it quiet, so Runa wouldn't hear. What was taking her so long? Mike stood up and came over to the couch, then flopped down beside me. I never really noticed before how womanly his face was. His lips were really full for a guy's, and he had the tiniest ears . . . I could feel how warm he was. It made the hairs on my arms stand on end.

"I'm serious. I'm just trying to help you out here," he said softly, picking at some loose threads on my collar. "Do you know that everyone talks about what a skank you are? Stuff like that makes me feel bad for you." He shook his head. "I mean, how would your old friend Tracy feel if she found out about you and Nick, for example? Think she'd want to know about that?"

"But . . . that's total bullshit," I said, sitting up straighter. "Tracy wasn't even going out with Nick back then."

He propped himself up. "Wendy," he said, smiling, "Sometimes you're so dumb that I feel sorry for you. That was just a lucky guess, and now you're busted. See? If you'd just be a little bit nicer to me, I wouldn't have to teach you these lessons. I mean, how can I trust my girlfriend not to be led astray by such a slut?"

I knew how red my cheeks must be. "You really are a fucking asshole, Mike," I whispered.

"Hey, I'm gonna make some popcorn, you guys," said Runa, coming in from the kitchen. She saw us on the couch and my flushed face.

"Oh, man, what's he doing now?" she said, putting her hands on her hips like a mom in a TV commercial. "Jesus, Mike, leave her alone and go to bed. You're hammered."

Runa was drunk now, and starting to ramble on about Mike. About his artistic talent, and how that could be his ticket to happiness and he wouldn't have to hurt himself in construction any more. How he gets drunk and cries about how sad and stupid he is, and how he's wrecked everyone's life and how sorry he is. And then has a jealous freak-out over nothing.

"I know it's just because he loves me, but it gets totally out of hand. I wish I could explain it. It's like this other part of his brain, the bad part, comes up with this lie about me, and it tells it to the good part, y'know? I swear, I can see this look on his face when it happens. And once he gets it, I know, even though I try, that talking to him isn't going to make one bit of difference—it'll probably only make it worse, because the bad part is stronger. It's stronger than me and it's stronger than him."

I don't mean to, but I kind of roll my eyes. "And *that's* why he hits you."

"Hey—you think I like it? Thing is, I can handle it—I can take a *punch*, for chrissakes. It's the other stuff that really hurts—calling me names, throwing things, wreckin' my shit. That's the worst, because I can tell he's still in the bad space, y'know? At least, once he starts swingin', I know it'll be over soon . . . it reminds him that I'm still there, that I'm real. I think he knows that too."

She lobs a bone into the chicken bucket, wipes her fingers on her jeans, and reaches for the bong. "But that's bullshit, right? I mean, what kind of a person am I if I don't stand up for myself? I can't wait to go to the station tomorrow."

"Okay, but I still think they're just going to tell you to go to the station where you live."

"Well, I'll do it then, goddammit. I'll go straight back up to Comox tomorrow morning and show the cops this eye and tell them everything. He'll be really sorry then."

I'm sure this is the time when a real friend would offer a place to stay, but I can't seem to say it. But Runa isn't waiting for that.

"And since you don't have school tomorrow, you're coming with me."

I wake up cold, with a thick, dirty mouth. We crashed in the bus because we were too wrecked to move back inside. Runa looks much prettier when she's sleeping—little pieces of hair are stuck to her sweaty cheek, covering her bruise almost completely, and her lips are wet and a little bit open. It's nice, and for second I want to stroke her head. Instead, I slide out of bed and go in the house. I have to call in sick for my shift at The Beanery, but it's no problem. There's a half-dozen part-timers scrambling to pick up hours in the off-season.

I make a full pot of employee-discount Beanery coffee

and have a shower, and by the time I get out, Runa's sitting in my kitchen, gathering her hair in a blue banana clip. "Christ, I'm a mess," she groans, rubbing her forehead. She does look rough. Her eye is starting to change colour from purple to greenish.

"Do you want to have a shower?" I ask. "There's probably still enough hot water if you're fast."

"Nah, fuck it. Pour me a coffee and let's jet before I lose my nerve."

It takes a lot of weed to hotbox a bus, but we're working on it. I pile some blankets in the stairwell so I can sit beside Runa as she drives. We're nearly to Duncan and working on another joint when she says, "I'm fuckin' starving. Let's hit the Doghouse for a seven-hundred-egg omelet."

She pulls into the parking lot, and I'm rooting around for my purse when she puts her forehead on the steering wheel with a thunk. "I don't think I can do it."

"Don't tell me you're paranoid about the Doghouse. God, we're not *that* high."

She looks up at me. "I can't do it to Mike."

My guts feel like cement. "You've got to be kidding," I say, realizing that this is what I've been expecting all along. "We're halfway there. Come on, let's get something to eat and figure this out."

"No, I can't." She's got her head down again.

I rub her back. It feels cold through her sweatshirt. "Why? Runa, are you scared he'll hurt you again?"

"No—it's because he needs me!" She starts bawling. "Because he needs me and he loves me and who will look after him if I go? What'll happen if they take him away from me and put him in jail or something? What will happen to the house? Where will I live? That's so fucked up! I can't do that shit to him."

Everything's got that extra-dramatic layer it gets when you're high, so I try to stay calm. But I'm standing there, trying to think of the best, most un-stoned thing to say, when I picture Mike leaning on the doorframe when he hears the bus pull up in the driveway. Holding a cigarette and trying to look tough, like he thinks he's Marlon Brando or something. The way his big lips will curl up at the corners when he sees me with her. The cocky, cruel assurance of a bully who knows he's gotten away with it again.

"Runa, I can't do this. You're my friend and I love you, but if you keep letting him pull this crap, I just don't think I can deal with it any more. Do you really believe you're that much of a piece of shit that you'll let this happen to you? Is this going to be your whole life—to keep going back to him and getting punched in the face because you're scared? Because you don't want to hurt his feelings?"

"Well, it's true and it's how I feel. We can't all just bail on everyone and totally change overnight into new people."

"Oh, great. Forgive *him* for smacking you around but don't forgive *me* for wanting to get my life together. That makes a lot of sense. Jesus Christ . . . " And for a second, I almost say *why won't you let me help you?* But I don't. I light two smokes and hand her one. It's quiet, except for some seagulls that hop and squawk around the dumpster.

"I know we're not going to Hollywood, you know," she says finally.

"What do you mean?"

"I'm talking about L.A. I know it's just a dumb dream we had. But I like it, because it reminds me of how we used to be friends."

"I never even said anything about that."

"Pffft. You don't have to, man. You look like I'm offering you a shit sandwich when I bring it up. I've got 473 bucks saved up that we're never going to use. It's like, not only have you moved away, but you lied to me about it. Who knows what else you lie about? Maybe all this time you've just hated me and couldn't say the truth."

"I could never hate you, Runa. Don't even say that."

She looks out the windshield, wipes her nose on her sleeve. "Do you know what?" She holds her two fingers out for another smoke. "The last time I left him, after he tried to kill himself and was in the hospital overnight, I went back to the house. There was a pot on the stove with the lid on. I looked inside and it was the macaroni and cheese that I had made two weeks before, the way he likes, with the cut-up hot dogs in it. It was all furry and disgusting. But there was something about seeing that pot that I had left on the stove the night that I left. That he had no idea what to do with it and so he just put the lid on it and left it there. More than anything . . . that fuckin' broke my heart. He needs me, Wendy. Do you know what it's like to have someone need you that much?"

I fish half the remaining cigarettes out of the pack, lay them on the dashboard, and pick up my purse and jacket. I reach over and jerk the handle to open the door of the bus.

"Where are you going?"

"I'm going back," I say. "Say hi to everyone at home for me, okay?"

"Wait, wait!" she wails. "How will you get home?"

"Who cares?" I shrug, and then I'm out the door.

I'm glad I brought my decent jacket, because it looks like rain. I put it on, jam my hands in my pockets, and start walking. I think about going in the Doghouse and eating breakfast anyway, but I should save my money to get a bus home. I think about turning around and going back, but I don't. Instead, I think about Runa's question as I'm walking across the parking lot of the strip mall. *No*, I think, *nobody needs me that much at all.*

Sugar Bush

metallic redhead's journal

metallic redhead **entries|friends|calendar**

May 27, 8:24 pm

I pried the door of the school bus open with a chunk of pipe. It was lying right there in the grass, so that's what everyone had been using to get in. It didn't smell nearly as gross inside as I'd expected. There was a bunch of shit on the floor where the seats used to be, blankets and old clothes and curled-up newspapers. Along one side, there was a row of old cabinets with tins of peaches and baked beans, packages of grape drink mix. Candle nubs and cigarette butts overflowed a few old tuna-fish cans. It made me sad to think of how much work I would have had to do to clean it up and make it nice.

I started with the clothes and blankets, spreading them out over the tops of the cabinets and the driver's seat. Then I started smashing things. I opened a can of sardines and dumped it on the floor, then tore open the drink mix powder and poured it on top. *Now* it smelled gross. I threw a can of peaches at the windshield, but it just bounced off and rolled away, leaving a trail of juice. There was some cherry brandy in the bottom of a mickey and I thought about drinking it, but it looked cloudy and skunky, so I dumped that out too. I found an unopened pack of Colts Mild and stuffed them in my jacket pocket. I got the lighter fluid out of my other pocket, and squirted it over everything until it was empty. My fingers were wet with it, so I wiped them on my jeans and flapped my arms around until they were dry. I backed down the stairs, lit a twisted-up shirt, and tossed it inside.

I wasn't thinking that it would really go up—I figured that the stuff inside would burn itself out and the sides might get singed and that would be the end of it. But it went up fast, just like in a movie, with crackling sounds and blistering paint. I stood there for a while, just watching—ever notice how fire does that to people? Flames are so pretty and soothing, almost like water, you could stand there daydreaming like you're at the beach watching the waves come in. It's peaceful, in a different way. But I had to get out of there, so I took off.

Looking out my bedroom window, I can see the smoke rising. It's darker than the twilight.

CURRENT MOOD: confused

CURRENT MUSIC: PJ Harvey *Uh Huh Her*

May 26, 7:14 pm

Sometimes life just fucking sucks. Being eighteen isn't going to change anything, except make me a bigger loser for not having accomplished anything in my whole life so far. I looked at the lake today and thought, if I had a boat, I could just get in it and start rowing until I got to the other side. I guess that would be Toronto. That would be far enough, and I could start over where no one knows me and I don't have a reputation and people would respect me for once and I'd get a job and start living my life for real. But I'm not going anywhere, and after all this is over, it's still going to be the same shit. I kinda wish I was going to university after all. At least it would be something different, and I'd get to get the fuck out of here.

CURRENT MOOD: frustrated

CURRENT MUSIC: Joy Division, *Unknown Pleasures*

May 25, 10:36 pm

My eighteenth birthday today. Got some pretty cool stuff from Mom and Dad. A new mp3 player (no, not an iPod, but what can you expect from old people? It still holds a shitload of songs though). I've loaded lots of stuff on it already—everything I do now will be set to music. I like that. My life is just one really long and boring movie, but at least it can have a good soundtrack. When I was a kid, I used to lie in the backseat of the car and pretend I was a character on a television show or in a movie, and that the songs on the radio were the background music (and also that I was going somewhere more interesting than the Safeway with Mom, like the airport or an orphanage or something). Lying in the backseat and looking up at the sky, the power lines along the highway were all I could see. They'd dip and swoop between the poles and when you looked at them upside down, they could kind of hypnotize you.

Yeah, aaaaanyway!

M and D took me for dinner at the Grill House, which I totally don't mind going to now that I don't work there. At first I never wanted to go there again, but now I think it's kind of funny. It used to really piss me off that I got canned for being late, like, only a couple times, but whatever. I'm so glad I'm not there anymore. Those people are all losers and I'm just lucky I got out when I did. I had the prime rib and the new girl was really nice to me and I didn't even get carded 'cause I was with my parents and they let me order a Singapore Sling.

The only shitty thing about this birthday is Kevin. I miss him so much! I don't know what I'm going to do. Well, I do know, but you know what I mean. I'm not sure it's going to help me feel any better. I just can't hurt his feelings when I love him so much. I wish at least one of my friends could understand that. Maybe someday, like years from now, we'll finally get to be together. The feeling I get when I think about what I have to do is something I can't really describe—sick and excited all at once. And then I just want it to be over.

CURRENT MOOD: hopeful

CURRENT MUSIC: Mastodon, *Leviathan*

May 24, 11:12 pm

Dear Kevin,

I know you'll never read this, but you deserve to know a few things. First of all, even though I've kind of been a bitch to you, I've totally fallen for you. I love you, I think, more than I've loved any other boy. You are sweet and nice and beautiful and I hope you can forgive me for hurting you.

That's the thing though—I can't even hurt you the way I'm supposed to. I know deep down that my friends are right, and that you're going to get hurt by me whatever happens, and that it's better to do it now, instead of dragging it out for a long time and *really* hurting you, like forever. I know all this, but it's not like it makes it any easier. It's like when you find out that there's no tooth fairy—it doesn't stop you from putting your teeth under the pillow, right?

I want to make love to you more than anything in the whole world, and not doing it is going to be one of my biggest regrets ever, I totally know it.

I'm so, so, so, so fucking sorry.

CURRENT MOOD: depressed

CURRENT MUSIC: Opeth, *Blackwater Park*

May 22, 6:57 pm

Grandma and Grandpa sent me a birthday card and fifty bucks—wicked! I used it to buy that awesome Zippo lighter with the swirly flower design. There's even a place for a monogram, so I'm getting my initials put on it at the key-cutting place in the plaza and picking it up tomorrow. I can't forget to get some lighter fluid too, so I can use it right away.

CURRENT MOOD: stoked!

CURRENT MUSIC: Isis, *Celestial*

May 20, 11:58 pm

Oh my god I hate my stupid friends!!!

Cherie invited me over to watch a movie tonight, and I was totally looking forward to it and to telling her about

Kevin and all the shit that's been going on. When I get there, Scott and Christie and Matt are already there and I think that we're going to have a good time. Then Cherie starts in on me, saying that she's really worried about me and this Kevin kid and that they've talked about it and they want me to not see him anymore and in her words, "just drop it."

I can't believe it. It's like they're staging some kind of a freaking intervention on my love life. It just blows my mind, and I can't even say anything to defend myself at first. When I do finally try to explain, Matt interrupts me and is all like, "He's a virgin, obviously, and he's like four years younger than you. What could you possibly even want with this kid?"

And Christie says, "Yeah, it's not like you're even going out with him. You're sneaking around in secret, and getting him in trouble, but you told me yourself that you're kind of embarrassed to be seen with him."

(I like how these guys were nowhere to be found when I lost my virginity in the back seat of a car to that creep Craig at his cousin's wedding—he was almost six years older than me and we did it and then he broke up with me, like, three days later over the phone. But I guess it doesn't matter when you're a girl. I tell them that and they're all "that was then and this is now" bullshit. I like how they're so interested in protecting someone they barely know instead of their so-called good friend. Really nice, assholes!!)

Scott says that it's different when you're a guy and that usually the first girl they hook up with messes them up pretty bad and that Kevin's going to fall in love with me if he hasn't already, and will probably kill himself or something.

I told him that I wish someone had let me know about this strange magical power I have over men a little sooner, because then I would have gotten a whole bunch of guys to kill themselves. But no one thinks this is funny. They keep at me until I'm totally crying and basically give me an ultimatum about their friendship if I don't break it off with him. I guess inside they're probably right, at least about some of it, but it's not like I'm going to give them the satisfaction of admitting it. I make them promise if I do it, that we'll never have to talk about it ever again, and that they'll never gang up on me like this. They agree, but I still end up leaving in a huff, because it's not like I can sit there and watch a movie after that.

Assholes.

CURRENT MOOD: humiliated

CURRENT MUSIC: nothing

May 18, 4:46 pm

I told Kevin my idea, and he really liked it. Maybe too much, because he got so into it when I told him about the bums living in it and stuff, that he decided that he wants to live in it for the summer and he's going to pack a bag and run away from home and then I can visit him whenever I want.

I tried to talk him out of it. I told him that bums could come back any time, like a bunch of them, and maybe beat him up or something. Or his parents could find him, or that my dad could find him and then he'd be in major shit. But it was weird—I've never seen him be so stubborn about something. I guess if my parents were like his, I'd want to run away too.

I feel bad. I was just thinking of one night, and now it's turning into this big deal, like when he took the pills. He's kind of being a drama queen.

CURRENT MOOD: guilty

CURRENT MUSIC: silence

May 17, 10:19 pm

My walk the other day with Dad gave me a good idea. If I cleaned up the old bus inside, I bet that Kevin and I could totally use it as our hideout. I could make it really nice in there, I bet, with candles and blankets and stuff. I can't wait to tell him—he could even take the bus home and tell his parents he was going out to a friend's house or something. I bet he could even ride his bike up here if he had to!

CURRENT MOOD: brilliant

CURRENT MUSIC: Strapping Young Lad, *City*

May 17, 8:28 pm

Kevin met me in the parking lot at lunch and we went for a walk along the lake. He had a bottle of his mother's sleeping pills and said that if we couldn't be together then maybe we should take them all and then we'd be together forever. He seemed really serious too, which freaked me out pretty bad. I told him that there probably wasn't enough of them for both of us and maybe we shouldn't rush into anything. There was a part of me that thought, why not? What have I got to live for anyway? I don't have any plans for the future, my life is totally boring, and I can't even be with the people I want to be with. But I know that this is just mental. It's like when Arleigh and I used to send suicide notes back and forth to each other in typing class when we were supposed to be doing our exercises and we would write about our funerals and how people would find our bodies and we'd look so pale and beautiful and what music we'd play when we were dying and what we'd wear and how the other one would have to make sure that we got buried in the right outfit and played the right music (even though she wanted them to play Evanescence, which I thought was totally gay). Besides, I told him, I don't want to die without us getting to make love first.

So I told Kevin that he should just put them back before his mom found out they were missing. I told him not to worry, that I'd figure something out. I couldn't completely waste an opportunity to get fucked-up though, so I put a couple of the pills in my pocket. I took one when we got back to school and ended up fully crashing in third period. Mr. Mowatt was all worried, but I told him I just stayed up really late working on a project and that I was fine. He let me go for the rest of the period, because I told him I was going to go to the nurse's office and I went to the cafeteria and had two Cokes and a Crispy Crunch just to keep from falling out of my chair. I'm still super tired.

CURRENT MOOD: sleepy

CURRENT MUSIC: Dimmu Borgir, *Enthrone Darkness Triumphant*

May 15, 5:13 pm

When I got home from school, I went for a little walk in the bush. They're going to cut down all the trees soon, I heard my dad telling my mom, because they're thinking of putting in a subdivision. It seems weird to think that in a few years, this place might not be here. It's not far from town, but in one short car trip, you're totally in farm country. It's weird to think that I might come back here when I'm old, in like twenty years or something, and everything around here, the fields and forests, will be houses and grocery stores and a Wal-Mart and shit. That'll be cool. It sucks as it is, because there's nothing for kids to do except ride their bikes around and play in the fields. I would miss the sugar bush though. It would be nice if they could keep that, just like a little reminder.

So anyway, I'm walking back there, smoking a joint and thinking, and I see the old bus. I haven't been around there in a while—when I came by once last year, I could hear creepy old-person voices inside and I got scared that some geezer might jump out and try to grab me. But that was when the weather was colder. I remember my mom calling the mayor or the alderman or somebody about it, saying that bums come and camp out in the bus in the winter and they should come and tow it away, but nobody ever did. I think they're still trying to find the owner, who I remember a little bit from when I was a kid. She moved in after the nice old man was gone and it was her bus that she parked in the bush, beside the sugar shack. She never made any maple syrup though, and she let all the supplies just sit there and the shed got all saggy and cobwebby and shit. Eventually one of the walls caved in and the whole thing filled with leaves, then snow.

I don't know what she did there, but she didn't have any kids. My mom said she was a lady cab driver, but I don't remember ever seeing a taxi. Anyway, she doesn't live there any more and the house was up for sale for a few years, but no one would buy it because it's pretty run down. I guess it's on a pretty big chunk of property though, with the bush and everything, so now these developer people are going to buy it and put in a bunch of townhouses or something. Anyway, the old bus is still there, sitting beside what's left of the sugar shack. I guess that'll finally get towed away if they're going to tear down all the trees.

CURRENT MOOD: reflective

CURRENT MUSIC: Patti Smith, *Horses*

May 13, 1:23 am

I can't believe it, but Dad let me borrow the car. Kevin snuck out of his house and I met him behind the Tim Horton's and we drove up to the point. I didn't want to fuck there (oh god, talk about embarrassing memories or what?!), but we fooled around for a while and then I sucked him off. Sometimes I think I'm not very good at it, but it only took a few minutes and I think that was partly because he was so freaked out by it. It wasn't bad at all. Usually I totally gag and have a tummyache afterwards. (Elaine told me she spits it out in a Kleenex, but I never seem to be organized enough to have one around at the crucial moment. Besides, how do you do that without being really obvious? I think if someone spit after they went down on me, my feelings would be totally hurt.) We listened to Opeth's *Damnation*, which was sooo romantic.

CURRENT MOOD: sexy!

CURRENT MUSIC: *Damnation* (of course!)

May 10, 5:07 pm

I stole some nail polish from the Shopper's Drug Mart today. (Burgundy Chic. It's really dark purple, almost black.) I don't know why, because I never bothered with that shit when all my other friends were really into it a few years ago. I was just bored, but I feel stupid about it now. Like I don't have enough to worry about without getting busted for stealing makeup? Having other people at the store see me, that would be the worst, though. How embarrassing can you get? I don't think I'll do it again, even though it was totally easy.

I want to be able to hook up with Kevin, but it's hard to find places to go. We can't just skip class and make out in the graveyard forever. I mean, soon it will be summer, and we can go up the mountain or to the beach, but there's always people partying around there, and the cops totally go there all the time. Besides, is it wrong to want to do it indoors once in a while? I don't even think M and D have any plans to go out of town any time soon.

There's a party this weekend, but as if I'm going to bring

him as my "date." And then do it in Arleigh's parents' bedroom? Eww—what am I, fifteen?

Then again, maybe if I come up with some big story about how I'm the designated driver, Dad will let me have the car. He's such a jerk about it sometimes. I have one accident that totally wasn't even my fault, and he's gonna hold it against me forever? Every time I ask now, he hounds me about why I haven't saved up enough to buy my own car yet. Um, because I'm in school, you retard? Geez. Besides, I don't want to buy some piece of shit old beater—I want a cute car!

CURRENT MOOD: indecisive

CURRENT MUSIC: Sleater-Kinney, *The Woods*

May 5, 8:00 pm

I went to McDonald's today with Elaine, so I waited for Kevin by his locker after lunch. He comes down the hall like a fart in a mitt, as Dad would say, with hair in his face. I kinda snapped at him. "I was on MSN for like three hours last night, waiting for you. What the hell happened?"

"I'm so, so sorry," he said and looked like he was going to cry. Obviously his parents are breathing down his neck when he's on the computer. They don't even let him have one in his room!

"Let's skip third period and we'll go somewhere and talk," I said.

"I can't skip third period—Mr. Freeman already saw me today, and then they'll call my parents and I'll be in even more trouble!" He was losing it.

I told him to fucking relax—everyone skips once in a while and no one ever phones home.

He met me in the cemetery. I had a smoke while he ate his nails. I asked him if he was going to let his parents run his whole life for him and he got kind of mad at me.

"My parents are strict," he said, "but they're not bad people." Jesus Christ, I never said they were.

But I asked him what he wanted to do. Like, if his parents say he can't see me anymore, is he going to listen to them? Then he kissed me. God, his lips are so soft and his skin is so perfect. I told him that I want him and he said he wants me too! I told him I really wanted to be his first, and he looked offended. "How do you know you'd be my first?" he asked.

I just laughed and put my smoke out on a headstone. I mean, come on.

"But why?" he asks. "You're three grades ahead of me and you're pretty and funny and cool. I don't get it. I keep thinking that this is like some big joke that you and your friends are playing on me."

I would have thought he was shitting me if I didn't look in

his eyes. Kevin doesn't have any kind of shell around him at all. It's kind of scary, actually. I couldn't even say anything for a second, because I was still soaking up how beautiful and cool he thinks I am. I guess maybe that's a part of it? That he thinks I am all those things, and not the spaz I feel like most of the time. With Kevin, all I have to do is to show up, and he's thrilled. I could tell him anything, and he'd believe it.

Anyway, we're totally going to have to figure something out. Making out in the graveyard is getting pretty lame.

My parents asked me what I wanted for my birthday today—I can't believe it's almost my birthday AGAIN! Fuck, I'm getting so old. I asked for a video iPod, but I know they'll choke on that, so I circled some other ones in the Future Shop catalogue as a backup.

CURRENT MOOD: old

CURRENT MUSIC: Mogwai, *Come On Die Young*

May 3, 11:22 am

Kevin's shithead little brother ratted him out for having a girl over last night, and his parents totally freaked on him. Of course, he admitted to it right away and they asked him a bunch of questions about me and he told them and now they've forbidden him to see me, because I'm older and such—get this—a bad influence!! I can't believe this. He just told me before second period and now I'm in the library and supposed to be working on my stupid history project and I don't even care. Seriously, this is soo retarded! His parents haven't even met me, so how the hell do they even know anything about me? I know something about them—they're fucking assholes and their kids are going to grow up to hate their guts.

And as if we're going to stop seeing each other. This is not over. This is not over. THIS IS NOT OVER.

CURRENT MOOD: rage

CURRENT MUSIC: bullshit library quiet

May 2, 11:09 pm

Tonight, Kevin's parents went for dinner at a friend's house and he and his little brother Brandon stayed home. I came over and we put the kid downstairs with a DVD and some pop and chips (which he's usually only allowed to have on weekends) and he and I went upstairs to his bedroom to "do homework"—ha ha! After a few minutes of making out, I got his shirt off. His chest was pale and completely smooth; his nipples were small and pink, like the inside of a seashell. I ran my hands all over him. I stroked his chest and he shivered all over. I took off my shirt and my bra then and we made out with our chests pressed together. It felt really good, his skin so warm against mine.

It's nice that, for once, I get to be the experienced and

cool one. I might act tough some of the time, but when I really like a guy, he's usually pretty cool and quite a bit older than me. I end up being in such awe of him that I kind of forget who I am (like with Gary, and Steve, and Mitch . . . hello, is there a pattern??). The stuff I say with my friends, or starting arguments sometimes just so I can win them, that kind of stuff all goes out the window when I'm going out with someone. The more myself I am, the more it seems to rub guys the wrong way. But this is different. I'm not scared of Kevin. I know that whatever I do, I'm going to have him. He doesn't have any tricks up his sleeve, and I can tell by his face that even though I freak him out, he's already totally in love with me. I wonder how long it will take him to say it? If I stay on him, I give it a week, tops.

CURRENT MOOD: powerful

CURRENT MUSIC: Turbonegro, *Apocalypse Dudes*

April 30, 10:17 pm

I called Kevin this afternoon, and of course he was home. I asked him why he didn't call me and he said he was worried that last night was just a joke or something, or that I was so drunk that I might be regretting what I did and changed my mind. I never regret anything, I told him. I'm wearing the pin I stole from Aaron's mother's jewellery box.

Let's meet up tonight and do something, I said. I was about to ask him to borrow a car, but then I remembered that he's not old enough to have a license yet. Yikes!

I caught a ride into town with Matt later and told him who I was meeting. I thought he'd think it was funny, but he seems to think I'm some kind of a child molester.

"Be careful," he told me. "You'll probably end up breaking his heart or something."

"What's the matter with you?" I said. "I like him."

"Fourteen is pretty young."

"Oh please," I said, "I lost it when I was thirteen to an older guy and nobody batted a fucking eye then. You're making me sound like the Marquis de Sade or something."

"The who?"

"Forget it." Matt is such a retard sometimes.

We met at the church parking lot behind the high school, and went for a walk in the cemetery. I brought a joint, but no booze this time, 'cause I'm kind of broke. I pulled it out and he started going off like the film strip that the cops show at the assembly every year.

"You don't actually believe all that shit, do you?" I asked. "You know that they just say that stuff to scare us." I took a toke and pulled him close to me. It wasn't a super-toke exactly, but he opened his mouth and I put my lips just barely touching his and blew the smoke into his mouth and he breathed it in. It was really sexy, and he let me do it three more times. Then we laughed and rolled around and kissed until my tongue actually hurt.

He's so sweet and funny, and I can totally tell that he's never had a girlfriend before or anything. That's kind of weird, but I like that he waits for me to take the lead on everything. Any other guy would have tried to fuck me right there on the grass.

I can't wait to see him again. I'm actually a little bit embarrassed about how stoked and excited I am. It's not like I want to be his girlfriend—I mean, he's not cool or anything, and he can't exactly hang out with me and my friends, can he? He's going to have to be like, my dirty little secret or something.

CURRENT MOOD: excited

CURRENT MUSIC: AC/DC, *Powerage*

April 30, 2:27 am

What a super fucked-up night! Aaron's party was last night, and I don't hang out with that crowd (no duh), but I've had a crush on Aaron since Grade 6. (Don't ask me why, because he's a total jock and an asshole and it's not like he ever even spoke to me in grade school—probably because I didn't grow tits or get my period until Grade 9.)

There weren't many people I liked there, and I was hanging out by myself, just drinking my beer and hoping Scott and Christie show up like they promised they would because otherwise I was just going to hitch a ride home with someone and watch my new Mastodon DVD.

After a while, Aaron came over to me, and he was pretty drunk. He was actually *really* drunk, I discovered, because he started telling me how happy he was that I came to the party. Like he gave a shit.

"Your hair's really red. When'd it get so red?" he says.

"I dyed it."

"It's really soft too . . . Wow, look at how red and shiny it is."

I was glad I wore it down for once—yes, because I am a sucker.

"Let's go to my room and talk," he said. I figured if Scott and Christie showed up, maybe they'd see my shoes by the door and know I was there.

So, we were in his room, making out and taking our clothes off, and I couldn't believe how hairy his back was! It was like an old guy's! Then he clambered on top of me and was barely even moving. I pushed him off me and got on top, hoping that my pretty hair would revive him. I'm riding away and going nowhere when he goes completely soft and makes a little *snork* sound. He was totally passed out! Call me old-fashioned, but I take it as a major insult when someone I'm fucking falls asleep on me.

I was pissed off, so I got dressed and sat on the edge of the bed for a while. Then I started rooting around in his stuff, but his room was a gross messy boy room, so it's not like I wanted to dig around too much. Across the hall was his mom and dad's room, so I went in there and had a look around. I took a couple of interesting-looking things from the jewellry box (nothing too fancy—a pin made out of an old spoon and a pair of gold butterfly earrings). I got nervous after that, so I had a quick look for Christine and Scott and decided to split. I was on my way out, panties stuffed in the pocket of my jeans, when I saw them. These two kids all hunched up in the corner sipping beer like they're in front of a fucking firing squad. (Don't even ask me how they got to this party, because I have no idea. A bigger, cooler brother or sister, I'm guessing.) They look hopeless, but the one without the glasses has the softest looking skin I've ever seen. The light is hitting him right or something because he turns his head to me, and time slows right down, and as he turns the light moves to behind him a bit and his long blond hair is making like, I swear to god, a fuckin' halo around his head, and I guess I must be smiling as I think this, because he smiles back at me and that's it. I'm just totally in love.

His name is Kevin, it turns out, and he's in Grade 9. I asked him if he wanted to go for a smoke and he said he didn't smoke. I told him to come with me anyway. We went outside and I had a smoke and another beer. He's so young looking, but gorgeous. His skin is like a baby's, and his eyes are really blue, with long fluttery girly eyelashes. It kind of freaks me out how sexy I think he is. I can usually barely stand guys my own age, much less younger. I was getting pretty drunk, so I stroked his hair, which is as soft as it looks, long and straight with lots of blonde sun streaks. He looks like a baby metalhead who hasn't figured out how to be scary yet, in his little jeans and his Lamb of God T-shirt.

I gave him some of my beer. He looked at me with this look that was so totally cute and innocent, it melted my fucking heart. I leaned over and kissed him, and he came back at me with way too much gusto, all awkward and pushing forward with his head, but he figured it out after a minute or two. He tasted like Kool-aid, I swear to god. My pussy was so wet I was worried it was going to leave a spot on my jeans (plus I still had my panties in my pocket!!).

We kissed like that for a long time, and he didn't try to touch my boobs or anything. I could feel his hard-on pressing up against me though.

After a while, he looked at his watch and said he had to go. It turned out he had to be home by his curfew! His parents are pretty strict, so he's got a whole bunch of rules. Everything he told me just made me want to corrupt him. I just wanted to drag him into the bushes and fuck his brains out. Anyway, we exchanged phone numbers and he promised to call me tomorrow.

Okay, must sleep now, so loaded and *tirrrrreeeeeddd!*

CURRENT MOOD: sleepy

CURRENT MUSIC: snoring

April 28, 6:04 pm

My dad asked me this afternoon if I wanted to go for a walk. How random is that? We used to go for walks all the time, but we never really do anymore. I said okay, but mostly just to get away from Mom. She looked like she might be planning some lame housework project for me. Besides, I needed a ride to the party tomorrow night, so I figured it couldn't hurt to throw the old man a bone.

We walked back to the bush and listened to the birds and stuff. My dad saw a fox, but as usual, I totally missed it.

We used to walk back there all the time. Even when I got a little older, I used to like to walk back there by myself, just to think or smoke, or whatever. I remember when we called it the sugar bush instead of just the bush because there was an old dude back here who used to make his own maple syrup.

My dad brought me back when the sap was running one March. We always used to go to the main sugar bush, a real one, that was only a few miles away. They did all the regular stuff there like sleigh rides and demonstrations of how they made the syrup and how the Indians used to do it and stuff, and Mom would always buy a gallon jug at the shop at the end of the tour and Dad and I would get to split a package of sugar candy in the little maple leaf shapes. Yum!

But the one just back from the house was way sketchier. The man made the syrup himself and he did it all the old-fashioned way: with the steel buckets and tapping the trees, then boiling everything down in a big galvanized tub in the sugar shack. It was pretty awesome. And it smelled really good too. I don't even remember that guy's name, but I remember he had a big white beard and he was really nice, too. He explained everything to me in a little-kid way, like a skinny Santa Claus. He poured all the sap into the big tub and told me how it took lots and lots of gallons of sap just to make a little bit of syrup. The shed was smoky, but nice. And the snow was still on the ground, but a lot of it was tramped down in paths from the shed to the trees and back and all melted around the shed.

I guess that guy died or something, because the shack is all fallen apart now, and that old school bus is back there beside it. There's a wire fence too, that marks the property line, and it's easy enough to climb over, but my dad and I don't bother. We just go sideways, past the pond and over towards the Chalykoff farm, where they have a bunch of rusty old tractors sitting back there, and then back up towards home on the next sideroad.

CURRENT MOOD: nostalgic

CURRENT MUSIC: Slayer, *Reign in Blood*

April 27, 9:49 pm

I can't wait until school is finished! It's so awesome that I'll be finished for good—which is seriously freaking my parents out, because I've decided not to go to university. Not yet anyway. I haven't figured out what I want to do, although I'm pretty sure it doesn't involve taking a bunch of stupid courses, getting drunk on Smirnoff Ice and date-raped at parties, and then flunking out after the first year anyway because I was too hung over to do my homework. Which is what university looks like to me. My teachers and guidance counselors are a little worried too, because they don't want to see my talents wasted, being such a bright girl and all. (God, I really hate the word "bright." It's a word that old guys, like my teachers, use when they can't deal with a girl who's actually smart. Like, does anyone ever describe a boy as "bright" unless they're still in diapers?)

I don't know what I'm going to do. I guess I'll get

another waitressing job (although I'd like to be a hostess, because that's super-easy and the girls who do that are always the most retarded sluts, which means I could go to work totally high and it wouldn't even matter).

CURRENT MOOD: impatient

CURRENT MUSIC: Sonic Youth, *Rather Ripped*

April 26, 7:14 pm

Started a new locked livejournal today. I've been looking over my old public lj and decided that I need to stop being such a gaylord. I guess there's a part of me that's scared someone will read this and I'll either get in major shit (yes, mom, I'm talking to you, you fuckin' nosy cow), or make fun of my feelings or whatever. But it's important to keep what Mrs. Norton called a "comprehensive document" in English class the other day. Sometimes famous writers have kept journals for most of their lives and then they get published later, like after they're dead. I guess I could handle being totally humiliated after I'm dead. But I'd rather be humiliated for something interesting! Not like these little gems from my old journal . . . "I slept in super late. Mom drove me to the mall with Cherie. I bought a new jean skirt at AE, which Mom said was too short and was all pissy and wanted me to take it back and we had a big fight. Then she made homemade macaroni and cheese for dinner and I stopped being mad at her." Gee, that's really fascinating. How am I ever going to be a world-famous writer with stuff like that? So from now on, I'm going to put it all down and try not to be afraid of getting caught. So yeah. Hang on to your nutsacs.

CURRENT MOOD: dreaming

CURRENT MUSIC: The Velvet Underground

Chicken Shack

Summer 1991

Craig Thomas asked me out right at the end of the school year. He had gone out with Anne for a couple months in Grade 9, but other than that, I didn't really know him that well. One minute I'm at some party and he says he likes my Neil Young shirt, the next minute, he phones me up out of the blue and asks me to go to a baseball game. I hate baseball, but I went anyway. Later, when we were making out in the parking lot, he told me he'd liked my shirt because I wasn't wearing a bra. Still, he was an okay guy. He was working at the lumberyard that summer, and making pretty good money too.

Me and the girls got fast food jobs for the summer. I wanted to work at the Black Forest again, like last year, but when the restaurant got sold to that mean old couple and they wanted us to wear those Oktoberfest beer-wench uniforms, I was like, No way. Candace's mom managed the Chicken Shack, and Candace told me they were still hiring summer staff, so I figured what the hell. Wendilynn had already signed up for a summer of flipping burgers, Anne was making tacos at that new Mexican place, and Lisa was doing her third summer at the donut shop out by the truck stop.

The Chicken Shack, which is a total rip-off of Kentucky Fried Chicken, isn't a great job by any stretch of the imagination, but it's the only place I know of that lets the staff take home free food. Whatever chicken is left at the end of the night, we either have to throw out or take home with us. We're supposed to try and finish the night with nothing left over, of course, but if someone comes in right before closing and wants a Snak Pak, we have to cook a whole tray of chicken—something about the "full and even loading of the fryers." I always save the honey-garlic wings for my dad 'cause they're his favourite, even though they make his ulcer act up. The rest of the chicken I just pack up and take to parties or wherever I'm going that night. Now, when everyone sees me pull up, they cheer, *Here comes the chicken lady!* Har-dee-har. Between that and the creepy customers who make jokes about "big breasts" and "juicy thighs," it's a real laugh riot.

The first week I worked there, Mrs. MacDonald—Candace's mom—made me clean out the grease trap. There's a giant sink in the back, and when the frozen chicken pieces come out of the freezer, the cook has to dump them in the sink and run cold water over them while they thaw. Under the sink is the grease trap—a metal box-thing that catches the gunk so it doesn't clog the pipes.

Mrs. MacDonald gave me a pair of rubber gloves and a bottle of cleaner that she warned me not to get on my skin. She told me that a couple of years ago one girl got a bad chemical burn when she tried to clean the grease trap in a half-top.

I was crawling around on the greasy floor under the sink forever, trying to pull the lid off the box. When I finally did, I almost threw up right there. It was full of rotten chicken fat and bits of bone and stuff. It smelled like death and puke and hell. The box doesn't come right off, so I had to scoop out all the crap with a little cup and dump it into a bucket. Then I had to close it all up again and run the super-corrosive cleaner through the drains. I found out later that the only time the grease trap ever gets emptied is when there's a new trainee.

Depending on what our shifts are like, sometimes one of the girls will come and visit me during work, or I'll go visit them. The best is when we go visit Anne at the Casa Mexicana. We're all crazy for tacos, just because it's something new. Anne always gives us tons of free stuff if her manager isn't around. This one time, we all had the day off except Anne, so we smoked some hash and went to the Casa to bug her. We ended up totally pigging out and acting like total spazzes. Her manager came over and told us we'd better settle down or we'd have to leave. Wendilynn grabbed her fajita, pointed it at him like a gun, and said in this super-serious voice, "A grilled chicken burrito, when handled properly and with the right amount of agility, can be a frightening thing." I just about pissed my pants, I was laughing so hard. Anne totally got in trouble for that later, which made me feel bad. Wen is such a nut sometimes. I don't know where she comes up with this shit. I love the way she's not scared of anything and likes to freak everyone out. People think she's really weird, but she gets straight-A's without hardly even trying. One time, in biology class, she asked Mr. Briggs if the human body was fit for consumption. Everyone was like, *Ewww!* Then Gary Emmett made some stupid comment and that was that. But you see what I mean, right? She's totally insane, but she's my best friend.

❧

Craig was not turning out to be the best boyfriend in the history of the world. For one thing, he's kind of dumb. I'm no Einstein or anything, but come on. I mean, the guy says stuff like "liberry" for "library" and "drownded" for "drowned." Also, he's really putting pressure on me to do it with him. He so doesn't get that I'd be way more into the idea if he'd just let up for, like, five seconds already. The minute we're alone at a party or in the movie theatre, he's instantly messing around with the top button on my jeans. It makes me feel weird, because I know he's done it before, and I know I'm sixteen and most girls my age have already done it like a hundred times. And it's not like I haven't done practically everything else, so what's the big deal, right? I dunno, something keeps stopping me. Maybe it's just the guys I've gone out with. We have a good time together and they seem to like me and everything, and then when we start fooling around, it's like they go all retarded. They're so pushy. It's not like I kind of imagined things would be when I was younger. I just don't want it to be like this big goal for them, y'know? I don't want Craig to paw me if all he's thinking about is getting off, I want it to be because we really like each other, because it feels good for both of us, because it *evolves*, you know? Okay, now I'm being a total loser. Forget it.

❧

One day, it was getting close to four o'clock, the end of my day shift at the Shack, when these huge clouds started rolling in. They were so dark and had this greenish cast to them that was super scary. The air got that still and staticky feeling like it does before a big storm.

Candace was covering a shift that her mom couldn't work. She was the worst employee ever—I guess because she knew her mom wouldn't fire her. She only came in when a shift needed covering anyway. From what I could tell, Candace spent most of her summer working on her tan. She told me all her weird tanning tricks, like plugging a fan in the outlet on the deck so she didn't get too hot. She always frosted her hair and wore really thick pale lipstick too, so she'd look even darker. It was weird, but whatever. She had been really chubby in Grade 9 and had lost a lot of weight, so I think she wanted to show it off. Some girls said she was a skank, but she always seemed okay to me.

Chris, the fry cook, said he was going for a smoke break before the rain started. "Let's go for a smoke break too," Candace said.

"But then there won't be anyone out front."

"No shit, Sherlock. Get me a marker."

Candace made a "back in five minutes" sign for the door and cranked her Jane's Addiction CD. Her mom would have totally killed us if she knew.

By the time we were ready to go out, it had already started pouring. Candace took off her work shirt and her shoes and her visor and threw them on the lid of the freezer. "C'mon," she said, "let's go get clean." It had been so hot all day and I felt so stinky and greasy. I took my stuff off too and rolled up the legs of my beige polyester pants.

It was dark out for the middle of the day. Candace and I ran around the back parking lot in our bras, yelling like freaks. The rain just made me feel slimier at first, but after a while I got used to it and then the wetter I got, the better it felt. I could just feel all that dirty chicken grease running off me, out of my hair. Chris smoked his cigarette sitting on a milk crate in the doorway, watching and laughing. After a while, the rain made everything so clean that you couldn't even smell the dumpster any more.

Lisa's parents went on holiday for two weeks in July, so we were crashing there a lot. Lisa decided to have a party while they were away. I had to work until close on Saturday, but I promised to come right after and bring chicken with me.

Craig was going to meet me there because he only lives a few minutes from Lisa's.

How come, the bigger of a hurry you are to get out of somewhere, the longer and more boring it's going to be? Work was so slow, and I stood around with my thumb up my ass all day waiting for it to end. Then sure enough, right before close, a bunch of people came in and ordered buckets, and salads, and boxes of fries.

I was running around in the back, packing up mini cheesecakes and styrofoam tubs of gravy while Chris loaded the cookers with more chicken. People get upset when you tell them their chicken's going to take twenty minutes, but they get even more upset if they think it's been sitting in the steam cabinet for five hours. You can't win.

Anyway, so I'm about to load in some new fries when I see that there's all this crap floating in the fry oil: bits of old fry and breadcrumbs and stuff. It's always so scummy by Saturday, because we only change the oil on Sunday nights. I grabbed the little mesh strainer thing that we use to scoop out the bits. I kept glancing through the pass-through window to the front while I'm doing it, keeping an eye on my crabby customers and hoping no more come in, when I accidentally dragged the knuckle of my index finger through the hot oil. It didn't even really hurt at first, just felt weird. Then it hurt *a lot*. I quickly wrapped a rag around it, loaded the fries, and got Chris to help me pack the chicken. Then I asked him to take the stuff out to the customers, and ran to the bathroom. Chris locked the door before any more customers could come in and helped me wrap a bunch of gauze around it.

"Man," he said, "that's really swollen. It's like one giant blister."

"I know. It's making me barf—just cover it up already. I've got a party to get to."

I walk into Lisa's kitchen with a bucket of chicken, and then make a second trip to the car for my knapsack. I thought for sure I was going to get in an accident on the way, because my right hand is just screaming and I couldn't really hold the wheel.

Nevermind is blasting, as usual. It's pretty good, but it's the only thing people ever listen to, so you think they'd be sick of it by now. Anyway, I'm more into stuff like Neil Young and Janis Joplin. In fact, I read somewhere that Southern Comfort was Janis's favourite drink, and that's why I have a twenty-sixer of it in my knapsack. I crack it open and wash down a couple Tylenols that Lisa brings me. Soon my finger doesn't hurt as much, and everyone makes me take off the gauze so they can see it. They all want to touch it.

"How come it's not crispy?" Anne asks.

"Because I didn't batter it first, you retard."

I don't see Craig anywhere, which is weird, but I'm not too worried about it. I hang out in the kitchen for a bit, drinking and talking. Then I bum a cigarette and go out in the back yard to smoke it. I'm fishing out a pack of matches when I hear voices from the gazebo. Lisa's parents have this super-corny gazebo thing that's all white wood and has seats inside.

I wander over to see what's going on. It's Craig and Candace trying to untangle themselves from each other. They're not doing a good job. I can see from the tag that Candace has her shirt on backwards. "Oh, man," is all Craig can say. Candace just looks at me and in the dark, I can't decide if her face is smug or embarrassed. Maybe it's both.

I turn around and walk out without saying anything. I tuck the smoke behind my ear and go back in the kitchen. I put the bucket of chicken under one arm and the twenty-sixer of Comfort under the other and walk out the front door. Nobody notices or says anything. I walk the few blocks to Craig's house, smoking and taking swigs from the bottle on the way. There're no cars in the driveway—his parents must have gone to a movie or something.

I start to lay the chicken pieces on the lawn, but when it takes eight pieces just to make a decent F, I change my mind. Instead, I use a piece to write "fuck you" in big greasy letters on Craig's living room window. I drink the rest of my bottle and toss the rest of the chicken around the garden and on the roof of the carport. There's only one piece left, so I wipe my hands on my jeans and eat it on the way back to Lisa's. It's a drumstick, too. That's my favourite.

Dish Pig

That's what they call all the dishwashing guys, not just me. Could be worse. Tammy, the hostess, gets called the "door whore," but we don't usually say it to her face. She gets really mad and her ears go all red and at first it was funny, but Tammy's such a bitch about it that it's not even worth it anymore.

This isn't bad for a first job. I could be sweating my ass off at the mill, or changing oil at Mr. Lube. Derek wanted me to come and work with him this summer, but I didn't want to get high every day and then spend eight hours standing underneath cars. I think it would freak me out. Derek's a good guy, but he smokes too much weed for me to keep up.

So yeah, dishes. I get a free dinner every shift, and people pretty much leave me alone. I like it that way. It's not like I was doing much with my nights anyway. Maybe in a couple years, when I can drive and stuff, it'll be different.

The one really good thing about this job is Amber—it's part of the reason I applied here in the first place. Although why I want to torture myself every day I'm not sure. Next year is her last year of high school, and I'm not kidding myself or anything. I just like to look at her. She's so perfect I can't even believe it. Seriously, she could be like, an underwear model or something. Half the time, if she's in the back and flirting with the cook or whatever, I can't even make out most of what she's saying, because all I can hear is the blood rushing out of my head towards my dick. It's pretty bad.

When I'm not checking Amber out, I'm washing the dishes. You know, when it's not too busy, like at the end of the night, and no one is going to ask me to come out of the dishpit and help out on the prep line and chop vegetables or anything and I've got just a few loads left to finish and I can put them through on my own time, I kind of like it. I can get in a zone with it. While each load is in the machine, I can get the next load ready, or stack and put away the load before it. I don't want to be doing it when I'm twenty-five or anything, but it does have a sort of rhythm.

Tonight is one of those good nights. It was just busy

enough. The shifts go by too slow when you're just standing around, and then Stu, the manager, comes by and finds some shitty job for me to do, like cleaning out the back freezer. But it wasn't so busy that everyone was freaking out. Most of the staff are already finished for the night, and they're sitting out front at the bar. Even though she's not nineteen yet, Rod the bartender lets Amber have a couple rum and Cokes when she stays after work. How could anyone say no to her for anything? I'd beat up my own grandpa if she told me she'd let me rub her ass for two minutes.

The jet trigger blasts off most of the leftover food gunk, then I stack each dish neatly in the tray. Silverware and some of the glasses can go in too, although I like to do those in separate loads. I stack everything nice and even, then slide them into the machine, pull the big lever that makes the lid go down and about a minute later, everything is done. I lift the lever up again and the tray slides out like nothing in it was ever dirty at all—all clean and shiny. It's hot too, so it's good to let the dishes sit for a minute before taking them out of the tray. It gets steamy in the pit when I'm running a lot of loads through, like a sauna or a big locker room.

It's a bad idea thinking about showers and saunas, though, because that makes me think of my favourite thing. One day earlier this summer, I saw Amber at the outdoor pool with a couple of kids she was babysitting. Seeing her in that blue bikini was the best day of my life. It was one of those stringy ones, with the triangles on the top, and the bottom that ties up on either side. From where I was sitting, I can't be sure, but I think there were little blue beads on the ends of the strings. But they could have just been knots.

I start thinking about what I think about nearly every time I'm alone: Amber coming out of the pool and rinsing off in that open shower area they make everyone go through, the water running down over her tits and stomach, and her moving around in slow circles so she can get completely rinsed off and her long blonde hair in one thick wet chunk down the middle of her back, and it being nearly black when it's wet, and before I know it I've got a major hard-on starting. I try to concentrate on the load of dishes in front of me, but I'm all twisted funny to one side and my balls are kind of stuck to my leg, so the whole thing's really uncomfortable, which of course makes my boner even worse.

I try to fix it, but I've got my big rubber gloves on and now it feels like there's a coupla pubes getting yanked to one side, so it's not a matter of just giving everything a nudge in the right direction anymore.

I have to run to the staff bathroom and get readjusted, but I decide to finish what I've started while I'm there. When I think about Amber, I go a little bit retarded. I want to look at her and touch her, yeah, but when I think about her tits and that ass, it's almost like I want to *be* her body. Like I want to be on the inside of her, looking out. I don't know, maybe that's how sex works. Fucking a girl is the closest you ever get to being inside one—for real, not just in her cunt I mean. Not that I want to be a girl or anything. I'm not a fag. I guess what I mean is, how can she look in the mirror every morning and not feel herself up all day long? I'd probably claw myself to pieces or something.

It takes about thirty seconds for me to finish. I flush the toilet paper and I'm about to wash my hands, but then I don't bother. Something about that "please wash hands" sign just pisses me off. Like I don't know any better.

When I'm finished the last load, I go out front and Rod gives me a Coke. Amber's there, waiting for Tammy to punch out and another waitress, who's still serving the last table.

"Hey, dish pig," Amber says, but she's smiling.

"Hey," I say, and sit down a couple of stools over.

I pretend to watch the ball game behind the bar and try not to look at her, tossing her hair around and eating maraschino cherries out of the service tray while she talks to Rod. Her rum and Coke is half full, and I could reach over and touch it I'm so close. There's a little pile of chewed-up cherry stems on the wet napkin it sits on.

And then I think, when she gets her stuff out of the back or goes to the bathroom, I'll just say something about the game, and Rod will turn around, and then I'll stick my fingers in her drink, and some of me will wash off. Then my come will be in there, and she'll come back and drink it. And some of my come will be in Amber's mouth.

But she doesn't go to the back. She just talks to Rod and eats more cherries as the ice melts. Then the other girls punch out and Tammy sits with her back to me as they count their tips. Then Amber stands up and picks her bag and jacket up from the floor and they all leave together without saying anything else to me. Rod picks up Amber's glass and turns it upside down with the others on the rubber treadmill and starts the bar dishwasher. I watch it as it goes in, then disappears.

Maternity Benefits

Alice took her cup of tea to the couch with the newspaper's classified section. She didn't especially want to find a new job. Carrying a baby around inside her was tiring, and her feet felt like bags of hot sand if she stood up for too long. Besides, most people seemed afraid of a pregnant woman working. Alice was certain that was why she lost her last job, at the shoe store. Crawling around on the floor and gathering up shoeboxes made her customers nervous and apologetic. It was hard to sell shoes to people who didn't want you to help them, and her sales dropped steadily as her circumference grew.

She was disappointed when they let her go, but relieved too. She had been daydreaming through her shifts, thinking about all the things she needed to buy and do before the baby came. If she didn't have to go to work, she could finally spend some time reading her baby books and getting the spare room turned into a nursery.

Jason came in with his Miller's Construction mug and perched on the arm of the couch, reading over her shoulder. He took three teaspoons of sugar in his tea, and the sound of his spoon going in circles made her a bit queasy.

He pointed at an ad. "How 'bout this one?"

"That's a pyramid scheme or Amway or something."

"How do you know?"

"Because I called it yesterday and they invite you to some 'seminar.'" She had suffered through one of them already. Alice and about a dozen other sad sacks were trapped in a windowless room while two oily looking men blathered on about financial independence and the freedom to succeed for nearly an hour and wouldn't tell them anything about the job. It turned out to be door-to-door vacuum cleaner sales (with a bonus set of steak knives). Alice didn't have her own car or the desire to haul a vacuum cleaner in and out of one. She hadn't actually called the one that Jason was pointing to but felt she could now pinpoint the scams from the wording.

"What's this one?" he asked, tapping one she'd circled.

"Looks like telemarketing," she said. "It's been in all week."

"'No selling,' it says."

"They all say that," said Alice. "Seems like telemarketers never actually have to sell anything, they just follow up on sales leads." She wanted a cool bath.

"You never know though," he said and went downstairs to his workshop.

Jason was home every day since he got laid off last month. His unemployment insurance was a decent amount, but Alice's UI maternity benefits from the shoe store wouldn't go into effect until the baby was born, and in the meantime, she could still bring in a few more paycheques. At least, that was what Jason said. He was taking some time off from his own job search to plan and build a grow-op behind their laundry room with the help of their neighbour Gord.

Alice gloomily recalled last week's interview at the museum gift shop. She had worn her longest, loosest hippie dress to hide how big she was, and then, right before she left, she put on a pair of old control-top pantyhose to try and mash the baby down. She remembered her mother speaking disdainfully of her great-aunt Edith, who wore girdles through all four of her pregnancies and one of her babies was born retarded, and of course no one said anything, but you never really knew, did you . . . Alice had patted her tummy and assured the baby that it was only for a couple hours. She figured it was probably the same as being stuck in the middle of the back seat on a car trip. It wasn't comfortable, but it wasn't going to kill you.

It hadn't worked. The manager had looked her over and known right away, although she was polite enough not to say anything. For the first time, Alice wished she wasn't so slim, then she might have been able to hide it better. And it looked like such a nice shop too: all the pretty little things for tourists to take home, lovely scented candles and soft music playing, light turning into rainbows through the leaded glass windows. Real class. When Alice left, the next interviewee was already waiting. A pretty thirty-something blonde, clutching a tan leather folder in her manicured fingers.

After Alice finished reading the comics and the horoscopes, she called the number in the ad she'd circled, and a friendly sounding man answered, named Herman. It was telemarketing: selling magazine subscriptions from an office. The good part was that the shifts were only four hours long.

"Look," she said, secretly hopeful. "I'm really pregnant. Is that going to be problem?"

"Oh no, lots of our sales representatives have been in a family way. We employ all kinds of people from all walks of life."

It turned out that the office wasn't far from their house, which meant Alice wouldn't have to take the bus all the way downtown. She could easily walk there in good weather. "What time should I come by then?"

"Any time this afternoon would be just fine."

The office was on the second floor of a small retail complex, above a vacant hobby shop with a sun-bleached For Lease sign in the window. Walking in the afternoon heat had made her sweaty and thirsty, so Alice bought an iced tea at the pizza place next door before she went upstairs. She opened the door to the small office. It wasn't air-conditioned. Three whirring fans atop a row of filing cabinets stirred the steamy air. Several men and women hunched at desks with telephone receivers to their ears, barely glancing up as she walked in. In one corner was a separate office with walls and a little window, and through the window Alice could see a man sitting at a desk. He stood up when he saw her and motioned her inside.

He looked like a Herman. His dress shirt was wrinkled and damp looking and his yellow striped tie had a grease spot on it. Herman sat across the desk from her and showed her the telemarketing script. He explained the offer and how to answer the different questions that customers might ask. The plaque from the Better Business Bureau was pointed out, and its value to customers was impressed upon her. The list of "sales leads" was a stapled bundle of photocopied sheets with names and numbers that looked a lot like a phone directory. The callers were all working on different regions, he explained. Today Alice would work on the Gulf Islands. It wasn't until Herman showed her to a desk that she realized she'd actually been hired.

Alice worked her first four-hour shift that afternoon and sold two subscriptions. Apparently this was very good for a first day. The pay was minimum wage, but if you sold a certain number of subscriptions over a certain number of shifts, you could earn bonuses too. Herman came out of his office and wrote her name on a big whiteboard with a blue marker and then rang a brass bell that hung beside the board. "Way to go, Alice," he said. "Everyone, we could have another star on our hands." He looked around the room with a broad smile and several people smiled wanly back at Alice. The man at the desk behind her actually clapped. She felt quite pleased with herself and then blushed with embarrassment at how easily she was made happy.

Alice returned to work the next day, better prepared with a big bottle of water and some trail mix in a sandwich bag. The four-hour shift felt longer—the subscriptions were a tough sell, and not just because many people hung up before you'd finished the first sentence of the script. The deal, or "offer" as Herman said, was that the customer got discounted subscriptions to six different magazines for a total of four years ("But never say 'four years'—always 'forty-eight months,'" Herman told her). It was a good value if you bought a lot of magazines at the store, but otherwise it was just a big pile of expensive paper. Alice thought of calling home and seeing if she could sell one to Jason. She wondered if he'd figure out it was her right away, or if he'd hang up on her before he clued in. If someone called her, and she could actually afford it, she wondered which six she would pick. She trailed a finger down the long list of titles. *Well, I'd get* Chatelaine *for the recipes, because it would be good if I knew how to cook more things, and I guess it would be smart to keep up on current affairs with* MacLean's, *even if it is boring, and that one's an especially good deal, since it comes out every week instead of just once a month. Gardening or farming magazines, they're dumb . . . oh,* Flare, *that one for sure . . . So that's three . . .*

"Hey, now, no daydreaming, you," said a voice behind her. Alice had been sitting with the phone tucked into the crook of her neck, listening to the dial tone. It was the man who had clapped for her yesterday. He had big eyebrows and a droopy, greying moustache, and he wore a full suit and tie in the stifling heat of the office. "Ha-ha, it's okay, I won't tell," he said. "Your name is Alice, right?"

"Uh-huh. What's yours?"

"I am Michael. What were you thinking about there? Maybe your little baby?"

"No, um, I was just thinking about what magazines I would buy if somebody called me."

"Oh, that's good," he said. "You make yourself familiar with the product; you'll sell them better. I should know. Did you know that I'm the top seller here? Once I sold nine subscriptions in one shift."

"That's amazing." She couldn't place his accent, but it had kind of an old-country sound.

"It is good," he agreed, nodding modestly. "That is why I always get dressed for work. One has always to be a professional. Customers cannot see you, but at the same time, they can know you and what sort of person you are, yes?"

"I guess so, yeah."

"So, you have a husband?"

Alice blushed, hoping this wasn't some kind of backwards pick-up line. "Yes, he's coming to pick me up later."

"Oh, that's good, a girl like you, with a baby on the way? You should have a husband."

"Mm-hm . . ."

"You know what else, my friend Alice? When a customer says no, you can't let them go that easy. Maybe they don't understand the deal yet. The longer you keep them on with you, the more they're going to feel like they owe you something. For all your hard work, you know? So don't just say, okay, yes, whatever, you keep them with you."

"Um, okay. Thanks, Michael."

Later that afternoon, one of Michael's customers called back to cancel the subscription he had bought an hour earlier. Michael's voice got louder and louder, until Herman came out of his office and stood there with his arms crossed. Alice hung up her phone and pretended to look for something in her purse. Michael finally bashed the receiver down. "Fucker!" he shouted. "You idiot dog fucker!" He threw his pen across the room, where it bounced off the wire mesh of one of the fans and rolled under an empty desk. Michael left the office, muttering in another language. Alice could see him through the window, pacing and smoking and talking to himself in the parking lot.

"Now, please don't misunderstand . . ." was the way one of the sentences began in her script. She had a hard time getting that one just right. She had to say it fast enough that people wouldn't interrupt her, but it also had to sound sincere, even though it was from the sheet. Really, thought Alice, it was the part of the script that should sound the *most* real, like a part she just threw in herself when she discovered that, Oh dear, people were misunderstanding what this great deal was all about. It was a line that stuck and played constantly in her head: when she was washing dishes or having a shower or just thinking. "Now, please don't misunderstand . . ." Sometimes she actually said it out loud, if she was deep enough in her own head. Jason had caught her once and teased her about it.

Sometimes Jason's teasing hurt her feelings, but she tried not to let on. It's not like she hadn't known what kind of guy he was when she started dating him.

She met him when the construction company he worked for did the renovations for the shoe store. She liked his laugh and how brash he was, even with his boss. Jason said out loud a lot of the things that Alice thought but kept hidden. She liked watching him work with his big rough hands. Still, she was surprised when he asked her out. What could he want with her? She was plain, even mousy, she thought. But from the first night they spent together, Alice knew Jason was the one. She felt so safe with him beside her. Their differences, she thought, completed each other, and he said as much himself. "It's like that old saying—you really are my better half," he told her. "Not like any other girl I ever dated—playing mind games, trying to make me jealous or trying to make me do a bunch of stuff I don't want to do. You're not like that, Alice."

And she resolved then to never be like that. In the last two years, Jason had been her best friend and her boyfriend and now he was going to be the father of her baby. Someday soon he would even be her husband, but they just hadn't gotten around to that yet. She said he was her husband, though, just because that made it easier for everyone. It wasn't really a lie if it was going to be true soon. She knew that deep down he must be as excited and scared about the baby as she was, but for the first time since she'd met him, he wasn't really expressing much of an opinion.

Alice's beginner's luck had run out. Most days, she was lucky to sell one subscription. What little enthusiasm she'd had for the job in the first place was waning as well. Each day the office seemed to get smaller and smaller and hotter and hotter, and she seemed to get bigger and bigger. She felt like her namesake in Wonderland after she drank the magic potion, too huge and ungainly to fit in such a tiny space. Her bum fell asleep after the first hour, and some days she got shooting pains along the backs of her thighs. Her fat ankles pulsed, like a heartbeat.

She was discovering ways to cheat for a few minutes at a time. Because the shifts were so short and it was unlucky to walk away from your desk if you were on a roll, the staff seldom took proper breaks. They stood up for more coffee, dumped in some Coffee-Mate, and sat back down again. They smoked at their desks with every cup. She wondered how they could stand it, in the heat. Alice was a little worried about being exposed to so much smoke, but she hoped it wasn't that big of a deal in the last trimester.

How she would cheat: she would dial all the numbers except the last one; if she did it fast enough no one could tell how many she dialed, or really slowly, as if she were confirming it as she dialed. Then she could sit there for a few seconds as though she was listening to it ring. Then she could cross it off and label it "no answer." Alice also liked to let the answering machine pick it up. She was supposed to hang up right away, but she usually let the whole message play out before she put the receiver back in its cradle. It wasn't much, but it gave her a short rest.

If Michael knew what she was up to, he didn't let on. He even took his smoke breaks outside most of the time, for the baby, he said. He tried to help her by offering her his advice and sales tips, but even his numbers had been falling. Alice started to resent his taps on her shoulder and his coffee-and-cigarette breath on her face, telling her dumb jokes and stories about his crazy ex-girlfriend until Herman came out of his office and glared at them. Alice wished she'd been colder to him at the beginning. Maybe then he wouldn't be acting like he was her new best friend. In a few more weeks, she'd be free of this place forever, so why should he care whether she did a better job? All Alice wanted was to get through the next few shifts, collect her cheque, and get as far away from Michael, the office, and that stupid phone as possible.

Alice felt the urgency of the baby's arrival. It kicked and shifted all the time, and it seemed like there was nowhere left for it to go but out. She was certain it was a boy and knew that would make Jason happy. She wanted to stay home; she had so much to do. The day before, she had had an urge to move all the clothes out of her closet and reorganize the whole thing, but only got as far as dumping everything on the bedroom floor and staring at all the outfits she might never fit into again. The only people who seemed to understand the importance of what was about to happen were the ladies who worked at the maternity shops and the Babies R Us, who quizzed her about so many aspects of her birth plan and her nursery colour scheme and her pain management drugs and her stroller options that she always left empty-handed, feeling confused and guilty.

That morning she'd had some funny pains in her tummy and wondered if she was going into labour early, but they'd gone away after a while. Jason had wanted to take her to the hospital and fretted so much that Alice wished she'd never brought it up. He was so nervous about her now, and Alice supposed she should have found it sweet, but mostly it was just annoying. He'd gotten himself into such a lather that he'd rolled a joint and smoked it even though it wasn't even lunchtime yet. Alice shooed him out once he'd calmed down, and he walked down the street to Gord's house to discuss more plans for the grow room. Their whole project was stalled while they waited for some special lights they'd ordered. She wished they were working on a plan to redecorate the nursery instead. Alice had been in the little grow room only once. It was painted from floor to ceiling in very bright white paint, like being inside a big glass of milk. It looked nice, and Alice wished it could stay like that, just empty. Maybe she could do yoga in it or make it a sewing room one day. She envisioned the hydro bills, the mess, the smell, the police. Jason had an answer for all of these things, but it didn't make her feel any safer.

He had left the roach in the ashtray. Alice smoked it while she got dressed for work. It might help her to relax, too. She missed smoking pot with Jason; a toke or two wouldn't be so bad for the baby, especially now. She hadn't counted on it hitting her so hard. It left her paranoid and agitated. She wished she could call in sick to work, but she knew that then Jason would think she really *was* sick, so she headed out, woozy and anxious. The office seemed especially small and hot. Michael seemed more jittery than usual, and his excited chatter on the phone behind her only made her feel worse.

After about half an hour, he tapped her on the shoulder. "Can I talk to you for a second?"

She turned around.

He leaned forward and whispered, "I cannot say very loud, but . . . do you have any pot I could buy or know where I could get some?"

Could everyone tell she had smoked some? Did she smell? "Why are you asking me this?"

"Oh, I don't know, I thought . . . I saw your husband. And he looked like he might, and you know . . . we're friends right?"

"No, I don't know," she said, insulted, but relieved it was Jason and not her that had been the tip-off. She turned back to her desk.

"Was he serious? How much did he want?" Jason asked, when Alice told him that night over supper.

"God, Jason, I don't know. You're not selling this guy any weed."

"Why not?" Jason said. "Maybe there's lots of people who'd buy there. Gord's guy will totally front me an ounce or two if I want to make a few bucks."

"Yeah, but I'm not working as you and Gord's pregnant drug dealer, okay? That's creepy."

"You're going to have to get used to this stuff, Al, especially if my business plan takes off."

"Business plan? Gee, you make it sound so classy." Alice stood up to clear their plates.

"Thanks a lot," he said. "I've been working really hard on this. Why can't you be excited about it?"

"Because I'm not very *excited* about a bunch of dirtbags tromping through here while I try to put a baby to sleep."

"Since when are all the people I know a bunch of dirtbags?"

"I'm sorry, sweetie," she said. "It's just that now, with the baby coming and everything, I feel like we should be good parents. I want to be a good mother, and I just don't think growing pot in our basement is that hot an idea."

"For chrissakes, Al, you think you might have brought this up before I made like, eighty trips to Home Depot? Besides, it's a fucking *baby*. For the first couple years, it doesn't even know enough not to shit itself. How much of a clue do you think it's going to have about what goes on?"

"You know what? Forget I said anything. Just do whatever you need to do, all right?"

"I never thought you'd turn out like this."

"Like what?" But she already knew.

The next day, Michael passed her a note in his shaky handwriting: *I'm sorry about yesterday, but I really need some. I don't have alot of friends so please help me if you can ok?*

Alice stood up and walked into Herman's office and closed the door behind her. Her hands were shaking. "Can you please tell Michael to stop hassling me? He seems to think I'm some kind of drug dealer."

Herman nodded, but didn't look very surprised. "I'll have a word with him," he said. "He seems to be under a lot of pressure lately."

"Well, that's not my fault. Besides, what kind of pressure makes it okay to harass pregnant ladies?"

"Alice, I'll put you at a different desk if that's what you want, but you have been encouraging him. Since you've been here, Michael's performance has really gone down—and yours has, too, in the last week or so . . ." He waved his hand over a stack of printouts.

"Oh come on, Herman. Half the people who come in here don't make it through their first shift. I've been here for every shift since I started, and that practically makes me employee of the month whether I talk or make the stupid bonus or not." She started to cry, like she always did when she was angry.

Herman fiddled with his tie. "Okay, Alice, take it easy now. I can see that you're upset. Why don't you forget about the rest of your shift for today?"

Alice looked at the desk calendar. August 22. Only two weeks to go until her due date. This month's picture was some ducks in a pretty pond, and next month's was an owl in a tree, but by that time, she would be gone and someone else would be looking at the calendar, sitting in her chair. Every morning, Alice hoped that this would be the day the baby would come so she could stop working. She had a new seat over by the whiteboard, but she could feel Michael's eyes on her during her shifts, and he glared at her every time she got up to use the bathroom. Even her old cheating methods weren't making her feel any better, and besides, now Herman had a clear view of her from his little window. She hadn't been doing very well.

She tried to cheer herself up, because she'd been assigned to the Gulf Islands again. They were her favourite; hardly anyone hung up on her, and many of the older people she called just liked to chat, even if they didn't buy anything. She dialed the next number on her list, a Mr. Moore.

"Well, I don't have much use for reading anymore, dear," he said after she had gone through her script. "My eyes aren't so good now, you see."

"Oh, that's too bad," said Alice.

"Yes, it is, dear. It's harder than ever to stay out of trouble if you can't see when it's coming. Now did you say your name was Alice? Like in the Lewis Carroll books?"

"That's right."

"Alice, dear, may I ask you a question?"

"I guess so . . ."

"Can you tell me when your baby is going to be born?"

"I don't . . . what? What? How . . ."

"Ah, I can hear it in your voice, my dear. My mother had sixteen children in her lifetime, although only twelve of them lived. And my wife, god bless her, gave me three sons and six beautiful daughters. So over the years, I've heard what a woman with child sounds like. It's not like any other sound in the world."

"I can't believe this. I'm having a baby in about two weeks. That's . . . incredible."

"Oh, now I wouldn't say that. I'm just an old fool with a big mouth. You take care of yourself, will you?"

Alice finished her shift, but Mr. Moore's strange trick had

thrown off her concentration, and she didn't make any sales all afternoon. She decided to work for another few minutes, until Jason got there. She couldn't make any money waiting for him in the parking lot.

She was on the phone with a Mrs. Blackmore, who was letting her opinion be known on the sorry state of *MacLean's* magazine, when she saw Jason's truck pull in. He got out and wandered over to Michael, who was sitting on the curb smoking. Michael handed Jason his lighter, and Jason lit a cigarette too. They talked for a few minutes, and Alice saw Michael point his thumb back towards the office and then Jason laughed. Alice looked down at her pad and *uh-huh'ed* Mrs. Blackmore. She watched the two of them walk over to the truck together. Jason reached inside the glove compartment, while Michael dug his wallet out of his back pocket. Alice hung up.

Alice called in sick on Thursday and Friday. She told Jason it was just swollen ankles and that she needed the weekend to rest. By Monday morning, he let her off the hook.

"Al, if you can't go back, that's okay, but you'd better go and pick up your last paycheque."

"Oh, honey. I just don't think I can take it anymore, you know? And I don't want Michael to bother me anymore either." She looked at Jason meaningfully, but he didn't seem to catch it.

"Right. I'll drive you over there in a little while, if you want. I promised Gord I'd help him pick up some stuff at the Revy first."

She put on her lightest maternity dress and her new white sandals. They were kind of ugly, but they made her feet feel better. She walked to the office, imagining the whole way what she would say—to Herman, but especially to Michael. *He thinks he's pretty smart, buddying up to Jason even after I told him to get lost. All for some stupid pot—what a loser.* She wondered what he had said to Jason that made him laugh so hard. Were they laughing at her? It wasn't really Jason's fault—he just wanted to make some money and be friends with everyone. She even found herself thinking about that creepy old guy on the island. She thought of going through her old call list and phoning him from home, telling him to keep his freaky mind-reading to himself. Everyone thought they knew her, but they didn't know anything. They'd find out today, though. She'd tell them all what she thought of them and their stupid jobs.

When she got to the office and yanked the downstairs door, it wouldn't open. She stepped back and looked upstairs, but all the lights were off, and there were no heads bent over the desks. There was a For Lease sign in one of the windows. Alice felt much too hot, and she ducked into the pizza place to get a Coke. She asked the man behind the counter if he knew anything about the tenant upstairs, but he just smiled and shrugged his shoulders.

Alice leaned on the counter and sipped her Coke and wondered what to do next. Then she felt a warm, whooshy feeling between her legs, like she had just peed herself. *Oh god, it must be my water breaking,* she thought. She looked down—wetness covered her bare legs and her new white sandals and made a puddle on the tile floor. She felt so embarrassed that her first thought was just to run all the way home. The water wasn't clear though, the way it was supposed to be, it was pink and sort of red. A line of red started to trickle down her right calf like a fat vein. Alice wondered, *Is this supposed to hurt?* but it didn't, just this funny feeling in her head and a strange loosening of everything in her insides and then she wasn't too warm at all, she was quite cold actually, and the tiles started to feel so mushy and soft beneath her and the corner of the counter she was leaning on turned into jelly and melted right out of her hand and the man behind the counter was coming out from behind it with a worried face and wiping his hands on his dirty apron and the last thing she remembered thinking before she hit the floor was *now please don't misunderstand . . .*